AF489607

THE EYES OF GOD

A COLLECTION OF STORIES

DANIEL M^cKENZIE

The Eyes of God

Calibration

The lab had the kind of cleanliness that erased time. No windows, no clock. Air filtered until it forgot it ever smelled like anything. On the far wall, a red light above the door blinked every seven seconds — the only pulse in the room that felt personal.

Mira settled the visor against her temples, waiting for the slight suction of the cups and the soft click of the electrodes finding home. The cable arced from the crown of her head to the console like a careful question.

"Baseline stable," Ana said, eyes on the graphs. "You're clear."

Mira exhaled. "Starting at twenty."

The fern on the bench reorganized first, as if relieved to drop the mask it wore for human eyes. The lazy label *plant* fell away, and what remained was insistence: fronds splitting into smaller fronds, angles holding steady across scales like a promise kept too many times to count. She could feel the visor subtracting — turning down the brain's running commentary until structure stood without narration.

"It's there," Mira said. "It's always been there."

Ana's pencil tapped the clipboard. "Self-similarity. Cheap way to build from a thin genome. Nature's been compressing data since before we had a word for it."

Mira smiled without looking away. "You always manage to make beauty sound like accounting."

"Accounting is how you keep beauty honest."

Mira tilted the fern gently; the leaves answered with tiny changes in torsion. Not metaphor. Mechanics. "I want water next."

Ana wheeled the cart closer. A stainless cup under a gooseneck lamp. The meniscus curved, a taut confession at the edge. When Ana blew across the rim, ripples ran like messengers, canceled, reappeared from the far side with second-hand news. The HVAC signed its name in delicate crosshatching. Even her own pulse, amplified through fingertips on steel, revealed itself as a traveling wave.

Mira's throat tightened. Not from sentiment. From relief. Seeing the pattern felt like setting down a weight she hadn't known she was carrying.

"Note that," Ana said. "Relief."

Mira resisted the urge to roll her eyes. "I'm not a subject."

"You're the first subject," Ana said, too evenly. "Twenty-five?"

"Twenty-eight."

The bowl of river stones refused to remain background. Smoothness decomposed into history: grain sizes broadcasting flow speed; nicks and concavities as ledger entries of collisions; a gloss that spoke of time under pressure. She picked one up. It was heavier than it looked — mass asserting itself against the lie of sight.

"Ordinary rocks," Ana said, not quite masking an edge. "I

still can't hear the choir."

"You don't have to hear it," Mira said softly. "It's singing anyway."

The corner camera watched them, a glass pupil where wall met ceiling. It didn't move. It didn't have to. Its existence had a way of lengthening pauses.

"Thirty-two," Mira said.

Ana's hand hovered over the dial a beat longer than necessary. "You push, you'll eat semantics."

"Do it."

The world sharpened. The bench stopped being bench and became a compromise between human reach, weight limits, and low-bid materials. The stool admitted it was a solution to torque and fatigue. The fern, stripped of its noun, stood on ratios alone and didn't mind.

"Δ equals point five six," Mira murmured. She had invented the index to soothe the part of her that needed numbers: a crude measure of how much her perceptual prior was being turned down. "At first, subtraction makes things cheap. Then it makes them rich."

Ana scribbled. "That line will kill at a conference."

"Only the first time," Mira said, and it made them both smile.

"Something mechanical," she added. "I want flow."

Ana produced a plastic desk fan from under the bench like a magician's slightly ashamed rabbit. Mira flicked it on. Blades that were formerly a blur resolved into a moving equation of torque resisting air. Currents braided into ribbons, shed vortices, tugged the fern with a signature Mira could almost spell. The motor hummed a chord with a wobble: one blade fractionally heavier than the rest; a manufacturer's indifference fossilized in sound.

Ana leaned in despite herself. "I'll never look at my fan the same way."

"Careful," Mira said, smiling. "That way lies madness."

"Useful madness," Ana said, and Mira couldn't tell if she meant it as a joke.

They took a break at the sink. Paper cups, lukewarm water. The visor sat in its cradle, faintly lit like a small animal at rest.

"How long until you let me try?" Ana asked the faucet.

"When it's safe," Mira said, and immediately wished she'd said it differently.

Ana dried her hands on the back of her lab coat. "You mean when it's safe for you."

"Don't make me the villain," Mira said, but she kept her tone light. "I'm being the adult in the room."

"The adult in the room has a cable coming out of her head," Ana said, and they both laughed, and the air thinned in a good way.

Back at the bench, Mira asked for a mirror. It wasn't part of today's plan, but the urge arrived like a tug. Ana fetched a square from a drawer and set it in Mira's hand with the ceremony of an offering she didn't approve of.

Mira lifted the mirror. Expected herself. Got planes and ratios instead. Symmetry held, but not perfectly

— childhood bike crash still in the tilt of a cheekbone; years at a screen in the set of the shoulders; diet and sleep, genetics and chance, all negotiating quietly and leaving their minutes in the face. Her eyes blinked back with no caption attached. Not I. Just constraints solving for survival.

She lowered the mirror carefully, as if it might bruise.

"Different when the subtraction is you," Ana said, almost gently. "Leaves and stones don't argue."

Mira nodded.

"What's the number?" Ana asked.

"Δ is point six zero," Mira said. "Enough for today."

Ana didn't argue. She powered down the amplifier with a sequence of clicks that was probably, to some engineer, also music.

Mira opened her notebook. *Perception is prediction. The visor subtracts the prediction. What remains is pattern. Patterns everywhere. Beauty = compressibility. Wonder = the relief of fewer bits.* She paused, then added a line she didn't entirely want to see on the page: *Ethics: when we turn this on people, what exactly do we take from them? If labels go, does blame?*

Behind her, a switch snapped. "Or meaning," Ana said, not looking up. "Maybe that goes, too."

Mira capped the pen. "You don't believe that."

Ana lifted a shoulder. "I want to know what's really there. Not what I hope is there."

The door beeped. The red light above it leveled into a steady on, then went dark again. No one entered. The room went back to being a sealed idea.

They logged the session. They put away the fern and the stones like props after a show. The visor cooled in its nest.

In the hallway, their badges opened a door that didn't look like a door until it did. A guard nodded the way people do when nodding is part of the uniform. The corridor smelled faintly of lemon and long decisions.

"Tomorrow," Ana said.

"Tomorrow," Mira said. She didn't add what rose in her throat: Let's keep it on stones a little longer.

Outside, evening had remembered how to smell: cut grass, a food truck's grill, rain far enough away to be a promise. Mira stood a moment under the split sky and watched students cross a green with the ungainly grace of people learning themselves. The visor was in a case at her side, quiet as a kept secret.

She considered calling her father, telling him that the spirals he drew on napkins weren't just pretty lies — that beauty really was compression, that patterns could carry wonder without permission. She put her phone back in her pocket. The words weren't ready. Some truths needed to warm in the hand before they could be given.

At the crosswalk she waited with everyone else. Red meant wait, white meant walk. Lawful enough to trust, for now. When the light changed, they moved as one and didn't step on each other, which felt, in its way, like a small miracle.

Tomorrow they would point the visor at faces.

Tonight she would let the world keep its gloss.

The Campus Walk

They crossed the campus at dusk, the visor tucked into its padded case at Mira's side. Ana walked beside her, silent except for the occasional scuff of shoes against pavement. The quad ahead was alive: students spilling across the paths, bikes carving diagonals, voices overlapping into a shifting hum.

"Baseline twenty," Mira said, lifting the visor.

Ana tapped her tablet, eyes on the data stream. "Vitals steady. Proceed."

Mira adjusted the strap and let the subtraction begin.

The gloss peeled away. Categories she normally snapped onto strangers — freshman, professor, groundskeeper — never arrived. What came first was older: the physics of posture, the grammar of mimicry.

A boy lifted his chin as he joined a group, syncing his stride without realizing it. A girl laughed too loudly, the sound shaped like a request: let me in. Mira hadn't known she knew this, but her body had always been decoding the grammar. The visor simply refused to hide it.

"Vitals?" Ana asked.

"Fine," Mira said, though her stomach was taut.

Ahead, two students argued. Without the visor, their words might have seemed defiant. Subtracted, the heat resolved into defense: storm fronts colliding, each bluffing against dissolution. Free will evaporated. What remained was weather.

Mira shivered. If she could see this so plainly, then anyone could. An advertiser, a politician, a machine. All you needed was the pattern, and you could play it.

Ana's voice cut in. "Weather, yes. But noise too. People pretending their storms mean something."

On a bench, a couple leaned close. Without subtraction they were charming. With it, they became choreography: the girl tucking her hair behind her ear, the boy's eyes pausing at her mouth. Predictable vectors of attention, old as deer in a clearing.

Mira felt a pang. The glue that bound people together was real, but fragile. If stripped bare, what would hold it?

Ana watched the couple a moment longer than necessary.

"Hormones and habit," she said finally. "Call it romance if you want, but biology doesn't."

"Forty-two," Mira said.

Language thinned. Conversations around them unraveled into probability flows: one sentence ending inviting inter-ruption, hesitations exposing where each person was willing to be wrong. Speech wasn't dialogue, it was math in duet.

A professor pedaled past on a bicycle, a stack of graded papers strapped to the rack. The red marks clustered in predictable places. Tired, but fair. Compassion surfaced in Mira before judgment had a chance.

Ana caught her expression. "Still good?"

"It doesn't make me colder," Mira said. "It just makes judgment feel clumsy."

Ana frowned. "Judgment's all most people have. Take it

away, what's left?"

Near the fountain, a child slipped on the wet stone. His father caught him by the jacket before he fell in. The visor showed the rescue not as heroism but inevitability: reflex braided from anatomy and urgency. The boy's breath changed shape as humiliation dissolved into relief.

The kindness wasn't diminished by seeing it this way. If anything, it felt more certain, inevitable as gravity.

Ana's arms were crossed. "A frog kicks when you touch its leg. Doesn't mean it's noble."

Mira lifted the visor half an inch. The world's gloss rushed back in — labels, names, the mercy of ordinariness. Students talking, leaves rustling, cars idling at a light. She breathed the relief of it.

"Plateau," Ana said.

"Plateau," Mira echoed.

But she couldn't resist lowering the visor again.

A security guard held the door for an older man. Through subtraction, it wasn't courtesy but adjustment: one body recognizing another's slowness and making space without thought. The kindness was real, but impersonal. The pattern closed itself.

Mira's chest tightened. If this was all pattern, then blame was flimsy, credit thinner still. The scaffolding of morality trembled like a house of cards.

Ana noticed the flicker in her face but said nothing. Her silence was harder than words.

Back in the lab, Mira set the visor in its cradle. The fern

looked dull again, stubbornly ordinary.

Ana slumped into her chair. "Well?"

Mira stared at the table. Her voice was quiet. "People are lawful. That much is clear. What I don't know is whether seeing that makes them more precious — or more disposable."

Ana didn't answer. The silence between them was safer than any guess.

Dinner at Home

The visor stayed in its case on the kitchen counter, its cradle light pulsing faintly like a pet waiting to be fed. Mira tried not to glance at it, but its presence pressed against her attention as surely as a third chair at the table.

James was already eating when she sat down. The lamp-light softened his face, catching in the fine creases around his eyes. He looked up, fork poised.

"How was it?" he asked. His tone was casual, but she caught the check-in underneath. He wasn't just making conversation.

She turned food on her plate without tasting it. "Hard to explain," she said. "Strange."

James gave her a look — the kind that asked for the truth without saying it aloud. "That's your answer when you don't want to tell me."

Mira tried to smile, but it faltered. Words resisted her. Instead, she studied him: the steady cycle of his jaw as he chewed, the rhythm of swallow and breath, the faint narrowing of his eyes before he spoke again. She saw it all as lawful, patterned. The visor wasn't even on, and still she couldn't unsee.

Ana's voice drifted back from the quad: *Hormones and habit. Call it romance if you want, but biology doesn't.*

"What?" James asked, setting his fork down.

"Nothing," she said too quickly.

"You're staring at me like I'm an experiment."

She laughed softly, but it came out thinner than she meant. "Maybe you are."

His expression sobered. He leaned forward, forearms braced against the table. "Mira, don't bring that thing home. Whatever it's doing, it's in your eyes. You feel… far away."

She forced herself to look again, really look. His smile — crooked, lopsided, the one she had loved since the first night they met — resolved into nothing more than ratios of muscle and light. Ana would have dismissed it as a reflex. But the warmth Mira felt seeing it — that hadn't vanished. If anything, without the gloss of ownership, it felt stronger, more certain.

"It's strange," she whispered. "The more I see you as pattern, the more I love you. Not because you're mine. Because you are. Because you exist at all."

James blinked, caught between confusion and tenderness. "That makes no sense."

"I know." She reached across the table and took his hand. "But it feels true."

For a moment the silence held them. His hand was warm, familiar. Her chest loosened, as though something clutched too tightly had finally released.

They finished the meal without much talk. Later, when James dozed on the couch, Mira sat watching his chest rise and fall. Breath in, breath out — the body solving itself. Ratios, reflexes, inevitability.

She waited for the feeling to collapse into machinery.

It didn't.

If anything, it felt larger, less dependent on him being hers.

For the first time, she wondered if this was what love really was: not possession, not story, but a quiet gravity pulling everything together. Wholeness.

She whispered it to herself, testing the word as if it might break: "Wholeness."

James stirred in his sleep, and she pulled the blanket over his shoulders.

The visor pulsed faintly from its cradle in the kitchen. Mira didn't look at it. For now, the rise and fall of James's breath was enough.

Ana's Turn

Ana lasted almost a week before caving.

She had hovered near the console every session, arms folded, jaw tight, jotting notes that never satisfied her. She mocked, minimized, but Mira could feel it building — the envy, the hunger.

That evening she broke. The lab was quiet, the air tinged with the faint lemon of the cleaning crew long gone. Mira was logging data when Ana spoke.

"Let me try."

Mira looked up. "No."

"You mean not yet."

"I mean no," Mira said. "It's not safe."

Ana's laugh was small, sharp. "You've been swimming in it for days. You're still here."

"That doesn't mean I should've."

Ana reached for the visor. "Mira, I've been with you since the first napkin equations. If this is going to matter, I need to see it. I won't stay your assistant in the dark."

Mira's hand hovered over the cradle. She wanted to refuse. She wanted to protect. But Ana's eyes had the set of someone already decided.

"Thirty," Mira said at last, her voice flat. "No higher."

Ana strapped the visor on, her hands steady. The console hummed as the system came alive.

The fern shifted first. Ana tilted her head. "Recursive geometry. Sure. Pretty enough."

"That's enough," Mira said.

Ana ignored her. "Forty."

"Ana —"

"Forty-five."

Her breath hitched. She looked at Mira, then back at the fern, then at her own hand.

"What do you see?" Mira asked carefully.

Ana's lips parted. At first her eyes lit with wonder, but the light cracked almost immediately. "You," she whispered. "Not… you. Ratios. Reflexes. Your smile — just a spasm of muscle. Your voice — a pressure wave pretending at kindness. Even the way you tilt your head when you're worried. All of it — scripted."

Mira's throat tightened. "That's not all it is."

Ana gave a sharp laugh. Hollow. "Isn't it? Look — " She raised her hand, turning it back and forth. "Flexion, extension. Signal, response. Puppet strings."

"Stop," Mira said.

Ana leaned forward, eyes fever-bright. "Don't you get it? There's no one here. Not in me. Not in you. Just the machine running itself."

Her voice rose, brittle. "And all those students you love to watch — their tender little dances? Pathetic. They think they matter. They think they're choosing. They're not. They're wind-up toys."

Mira reached for the console. "I'm pulling you out."

"Forty-eight," Ana snapped.

The visor clicked.

Ana stiffened. Her face drained of color. She pressed both hands to her temples. "Oh God."

Mira's chest constricted. "Ana — "

Ana's words tumbled out, shaking. "It's nothing. It's all nothing. I thought there'd be something underneath, some spark. But there isn't. Just pattern grinding against pattern.

Meaning is the prettiest lie we tell ourselves. Even love. Especially love."

Mira dropped the gain to twenty. The visor sighed and released her.

Ana ripped it off, threw it onto the bench. Her breath came ragged, shallow.

She stared at Mira, eyes wet, voice hard. "You said this was beautiful. To me it's death. If this is the world, then nothing matters. Nothing at all."

Her hands shook as she gathered her bag. "Don't ask me to put this thing on again. Ever."

She left the lab without looking back.

Mira stood in the silence, the visor gleaming faintly in its cradle. Two people had looked through the same window. One had found wonder. The other, a void.

The Fallout

Ana didn't come in the next day. Or the next.

Mira called. Texted. Left two voicemails that sounded too careful. By late afternoon of the second day she drove across town with the visor still in its case on the back seat, as if forgetting it might count as mercy.

The hallway outside Ana's apartment smelled faintly of old carpet cleaner and boiled rice. It took a long time for the deadbolt to turn. When the door opened, Ana stood there in an oversized hoodie and socks, hair matted to one side, eyes swollen from lack of sleep.

"Hey," Mira said, uselessly.

Ana stepped aside without answering.

The curtains were drawn. Light seeped around the edges as if it wasn't sure it was allowed. A half-eaten sandwich sagged on a plate on the coffee table. A glass of water wore a thin skin of dust. On the bookshelf, frames with family photos faced the room like small witnesses. Ana curled back into the sofa and pulled a blanket to her chin, as if resuming a position she hadn't left.

Mira sat in the chair opposite. She waited. The refrigerator clicked and fell silent.

"You disappeared," she said finally.

"I didn't want to talk." Ana's voice was flat, as if thrown from far away.

"You scared me."

Ana let out something that wanted to be a laugh and wasn't. "I scare me."

Mira looked around for a place to set her bag and didn't find one. "Have you slept?"

"Two hours," Ana said. "Then I woke up to the same pane of glass."

"What glass?"

Ana stared at the far wall. "The one between me and everything. It's not the visor. It's what's left after. People don't look like people anymore. They look like scripts trying to appear kind."

Mira folded her hands together and felt how performative that could look, even to herself. "Tell me."

Ana's gaze stayed on the wall. "My neighbor held the door yesterday. I used to think that was courtesy. All I could see was load sharing. One body calculating friction and time. My sister called. I played her voice mail three times. All I could hear was the intonation we learned in our mother's kitchen. Same cadence. Same appeal. Attachment routines." She shook her head. "I went to make tea and couldn't remember if I wanted it. Wanting felt like another reflex."

Mira swallowed. "That sounds…hard."

"It's empty," Ana said. "That's the word. I hoped there would be something underneath the masks — some core that looked back. But there isn't. Just pattern grinding on pattern." She shifted under the blanket. "I opened an old photo album last night. I thought maybe memory would save me. But I couldn't see my father's hand on my shoulder as love. Just grip strength and angle. We were both younger. That's all."

Mira's eyes went to the photos on the shelf: a beach, a graduation, Ana in braces, grinning. She remembered the way Ana had looked at the fern — skeptical even when beauty insisted.

"You're not a script."

Ana turned her head then, finally looking at Mira. Her eyes were red but sharp. "Then tell me what I am." She waited a beat and, when no answer came, went on, softer. "You went home to James and discovered something. I can see it on you. You're steadier. You found a word. I didn't."

Mira opened her mouth and closed it. She wanted to say love. She wanted to say the word without making it a sermon or a cure. The word felt like a fragile bowl. Handing it across the room might break it.

Ana looked back at the wall. "I keep replaying every time I thought I loved someone. Every time I thought they loved me. Ratios, reflexes, hormones, practice. Tell me why I should care about any of it now that I can see the gears."

"Because it still hurts when it breaks," Mira said. "Because it still matters when it holds."

"Pain is a signal," Ana said. "So is relief. That's not the same as meaning."

They sat with that. Outside, a car alarm complained and then gave up.

"Eat something," Mira said after a while. "Please."

Ana made a vague gesture at the sandwich. "I tried. It tasted like paste."

"Shower, then," Mira said, gentler. "Or walk with me."

Ana's mouth twitched, not quite a smile. "You're doing the human-things checklist."

"It helps."

"It helps if you believe in the human."

Mira stared at the corner of the rug where a thread had come loose and coiled into a tiny question mark. "Do you want me to stay?"

"I don't know," Ana said. "I don't know what wanting is right now."

Mira got up anyway and went to the kitchen. The sink

held two mugs with rings of old tea at the bottom. She ran hot water and watched steam lift — physics doing its quiet job — and found a clean glass. When she brought it back, Ana took it without thanks and without refusal, which was a kind of thanks.

They sat again.

Ana spoke into the blanket. "Choice is the first illusion to go." Her voice thinned. "I thought I wanted to be free of lies. I didn't realize I was made of them."

Mira reached across and touched the back of Ana's hand where it clutched the blanket. The contact startled both of them and then steadied. "You're not made of lies."

"You're going to say love," Ana said. "Don't. Not today. I can't hear it without hating you a little."

Mira let her hand stay. "Then I won't say it."

They sat until the light behind the curtains shifted from the color of dust to the color of early evening. The room grew cooler. Somewhere, a neighbor laughed, then hushed themselves as if laughter needed a permit.

Ana spoke again, very quietly. "What if the visor is the honest thing, and everything else is anesthesia?"

"Then we'll need a way to stay awake that doesn't destroy us," Mira said.

Ana breathed out, a sound that wasn't a laugh and wasn't a sob. "Do you have one?"

"I have a thread," Mira said. "It's thin. But it holds."

Ana rolled onto her side, facing the sofa back. "I don't."

Mira stayed until the first streetlight came on and the

apartment changed shape around its glow. She washed the dishes without being asked. She opened the curtains an inch and then another. When she stood at the door to leave, Ana didn't move, but she said, "Text me when you get home."

"I will," Mira said.

In the hallway, the building hummed its impersonal lullaby. She leaned against the wall and pressed her palms to her eyes until colors bloomed. On the drive back, every red light felt like a small mercy — lawfulness offering her somewhere to rest.

At home, James was on the couch with a book face down on his chest. He looked up when she came in, reading her face the way people do when they love without a theory for it. She sat beside him and let her head fall to his shoulder. For a long time she didn't speak.

Later, in bed, the ceiling held its familiar imperfections, tiny constellations of plaster. Sleep didn't come. Ana's voice did: Meaning is the prettiest lie. And another, quieter line beneath it that wasn't exactly a voice: Find a way to make truth survivable.

Mira thought about the lab at night — how the coolant lines whispered, how the visor's cradle pulsed as if it had a pulse of its own. She knew what she was going to do, and the knowledge felt like standing at the lip of a cold lake in the dark.

She texted Ana anyway: *Home. Here if you need me.*

A minute later, three dots flickered and vanished. Then:

Try to sleep.

Mira turned the phone face down. In the silence, she matched her breath to James's until it steadied. The thread held. It was thin. It held.

The Funders

The conference room was nothing like the lab. No ferns, no stones — just a long table under recessed lights and glass-paneled walls polished to a mirror sheen. Mira sat stiffly, the visor's case on the chair beside her. Ana leafed through a notepad she hadn't written in.

Two guards waited outside. Their shadows shifted when people passed the hall. The message was clear: this wasn't a meeting. It was a summons.

The funders arrived in pairs. The lawyer came first, shoes clicking against the floor. Behind him, two men in near-identical suits, followed by a woman with the measured calm of a diplomat. None of them offered last names. Their greetings were polite but cool, the kind reserved for things already bought.

Mira felt Ana shift beside her — not nervous, exactly, but braced, like someone facing an exam.

The lawyer took the head of the table. "Dr. Varma. Dr. Klein. Thank you for coming. Your work has attracted considerable attention."

It was the first time Mira had heard it called their work in this setting. Until now it had been the project. Or worse, the asset.

Ana sat rigid, eyes rimmed but alert. She hadn't said much since her collapse in the lab, but she had agreed to this meeting without protest. Mira wasn't sure if that was strength returning — or surrender.

Mira set the case on the table but didn't open it. It sat between them like an urn.

The lawyer leaned forward, smile measured. "We've reviewed your reports. Impressive. If this technology scales as you claim, the applications are extensive."

Mira's hands stayed folded in her lap.

One of the men cleared his throat. "Defense, for example. Interrogations finished in minutes. No false leads, no wasted time. A negotiator who sees every bluff before it's spoken."

The woman added smoothly, "National security would fund ten labs like yours. Probably more."

Mira let the silence stretch until the HVAC hum filled it.

The second man smiled, as though to rescue the pause. "Advertising. Imagine zero wasted impressions. Messages slipping past resistance, striking where it counts. Every time."

Mira thought of the boy on the quad, laughing too loudly for acceptance. The father at the fountain, hand closing around his son's jacket. Lawful patterns. Tender patterns. All exploitable.

She said nothing.

The lawyer's smile thinned. "Doctor, you've built a truth

machine. Strip away masks, reveal the machinery. That changes everything."

Mira laid her hand on the case. Her voice was quiet. "It isn't a truth machine. It doesn't show essence. It shows pattern. Machinery, yes. And once you see machinery, the temptation is to use it."

The first man raised his brows. "And you won't?"

Mira met his eyes. "No."

"You don't get to choose," he said gently, almost kindly. "Technology doesn't wait for conscience."

Ana spoke then, her voice steady but edged. "She's right about temptation. Once you've seen it, you can't not use it. The question isn't *whether*, but *how*. The last time someone built a machine like this, it was called civilization. Agriculture, writing, law — each one stripped away mystery and replaced it with something legible, usable. This is the same. The next lens. And the next leash."

The funders laughed, uneasily.

Mira turned toward her. "Ana — "

But Ana didn't back down. "You wanted honesty. That's honesty. Civilization is built on leashes. This will be no different. Useful, yes. Dangerous, absolutely. But inevitable."

The lawyer steepled his fingers. "I'm glad at least one of you sees the scale."

Mira's face heated. Ana's words weren't false, but spoken here they felt like surrender — as if inevitability had already chosen sides.

She closed the case with a click. "Then if it comes, it won't come from me."

The woman's smile held, but her eyes hardened. "We'll note your position."

Outside in the corridor, Mira exhaled, the weight of the case pressing hard against her side.

Ana broke the silence. "Don't look at me like that. I just said the quiet part out loud."

Mira stopped. "You didn't just say it. You made it sound like we agreed."

Ana shrugged, eyes forward. "Maybe the inevitability will make them think harder."

Mira stared at her. The words could have been warning. They could have been concession. She couldn't tell. All she knew was that in that room, with their eyes on her, she had felt isolated. Alone.

Ana's mouth twitched — half smile, half defense. "You'll thank me later."

Mira tightened her grip on the case. She wasn't sure if Ana had just stood beside her, or across from her.

The hallway stretched ahead, fluorescent lights humming like a verdict.

Mira Alone in the Lab

The lab was too quiet. Without Ana's rustle of notes, without her skeptical commentary, the silence pressed against Mira's ears. The fluorescents hummed overhead. Coolant whispered in the walls. Every sound felt amplified, as if the room itself were listening.

She placed the visor on the bench. Its black casing caught the light and warped her reflection into an oval mask. She rested her hands on either side, fingers trembling.

James's voice echoed: *Don't bring that thing home. Whatever it's doing, it's written in your eyes.*

Ana's harsher voice overlapped: *Meaning is the prettiest lie we tell ourselves.*

Mira swallowed. She wasn't sure which voice frightened her more.

She lowered the visor onto her temples. The electrodes kissed her skin, suctioned lightly, roots planting. The console's hum deepened.

"Sixty," she whispered.

The world folded.

Her arm rose from her side, but not by her. *No I am lifting.* Just torque, leverage, a vine solving for light. When it fell against the bench, the sound arrived before the thought. Ownership never came.

Her heart stumbled. She pressed her palm to her chest. The beat thudded steady, impersonal. Not hers. Never hers.

Breath came ragged. The visor subtracted even that: diaphragm contracting, alveoli exchanging gases, chemistry ticking like a metronome.

"I'm still here," she whispered. But the words dissolved into vibration.

The body wasn't hers. It was process.

Fear swelled. Chest tight, pulse racing. The visor pared it

down: hormone surges, muscle contraction.

Then grief, sharp and hot. Collapsed into cortisol, saline tears, a constricted throat.

Loneliness followed — vast, echoing. Subtracted into mammalian alarm, chemistry of social survival.

She clutched the bench, nails biting wood. Ana's voice cut through memory: *It's all nothing. I thought there'd be something underneath. But there isn't.*

Her stomach lurched. In the console's black gloss she saw herself — ratios, flaws, symmetry. An organism solving equations.

Lightning thought: *If suffering isn't mine, who suffers? Who loves? Who chooses?*

Her mind reached for anchor.

Her mother's hand on her forehead. Subtracted: heat exchange, caregiving reflex.

Her first kiss. Subtracted: dopamine surge, mimicry rehearsed millions of times.

Her father's spirals on napkins. Subtracted: compression, geometry. But memory gave more than math: the diner's chipped Formica table, the smell of burnt coffee, her father leaning close, grinning as he tapped the spiral's center. "See, Mira? No matter how far it goes, it folds back. Everything belongs." She had laughed then, not understanding. Now the visor stripped even that warmth, leaving only ratios circling endlessly inward.

Each memory gutted of warmth, left as raw mechanics.

She gasped. Sacred things dissolved into pattern grinding

on pattern.

Ana was right.

Her vision flickered. Her hands shriveled, veins raised, skin gray. She cried out — but the visor peeled it bare: not prophecy, only fear rehearsing its end.

The lab tilted. She saw herself gone, stool spinning slowly where she had sat. Again the visor stripped it: neurons simulating inevitability.

Her throat closed. Breath shallow. She felt already absent.

Silence swallowed her. Not the silence of a room, but of dissolution.

Thoughts thinned. Language fractured. She was glass about to shatter.

Ana's despair echoed: It's all nothing.

The void pressed infinite and uncaring. Pattern without center. Law without witness.

Her mind felt brittle. One more subtraction and she would break.

And then — something held. A thread, invisible yet unbreakable.

James surfaced first. His crooked smile, imperfect, human. Not hers, not anyone's. Just presence.

The warmth she'd felt at the dinner table hadn't been stripped. It was stronger now, amplified by subtraction. She had whispered wholeness then, tentative. Now it rang in her like a bell.

The visor pressed harder, testing her. Prove it.

More faces came.

The child at the fountain, breath caught between humiliation and relief.

The boy on the quad, laughter too loud, pleading for entry.

The professor on his bike, red ink marking effort.

Her father at the café, spirals tightening into geometry older than language.

Even Ana, curled under her blanket, eyes hollow with void.

All lawful. All pattern. And yet the thread ran through them — not in spite of the gears, but because of them. Love wasn't outside the machinery. Love was the machinery seen whole.

Her tears ran freely, and even as saline, ducts, reflex — they mattered.

The warmth swelled until it became gravity. Not metaphorical pull but real — binding bodies, thoughts, sorrows, kindness into one curve.

She saw then how Ana had missed it. She had stopped at subtraction, recoiled from gears, despaired at their blind turning. But the gears weren't blind. They carried one another. Every reflex, every kindness was not an island but a fold in a larger arc.

"This," Mira whispered, voice breaking, "this must be what it is to see with the eyes of God."

Not judgment. Not void. Only love written through the machinery, carrying everything, refusing nothing.

The terror remained, but braided into the whole. Included, it lost its teeth.

For the first time, she could stand inside the abyss without breaking.

At last she tore the visor off.

The ordinary world rushed back violently: fern as "fern," bowl as "bowl," the mercy of labels. She gulped them down like air after nearly drowning.

She almost wept from gratitude. *Chair. Table. Wall.* She repeated them like prayers.

But beneath the words, something glowed — patterns pulsing patient, eternal. She could see them if she wished. Ratios in the mirror, law in the ripple, inevitability in breath.

And she did not resent the gloss anymore. She saw it for what it was: a veil, not a lie. A soft cloth laid over a blazing lamp so eyes could bear to look. *Maya as mercy.*

She sat back, chest heaving, visor trembling in her hands. The fern looked dull again, the stones stubbornly ordinary. But she would never mistake them as merely ordinary again.

Her notebook lay open. She wrote slowly:

Patterns are real. But the Whole is more real. The void is real, but it is held. The doer is illusion. Love remains.

The simplicity startled her. Her father's spirals had pointed here all along. She just hadn't known how to read them.

Closing the case, she felt its weight in her hands — not just plastic and circuits, but the weight of crossing the abyss. She whispered to the empty room, "I can't unknow this."

And this time, it wasn't fear. It was vow.

The Dream World

James was waiting on the couch when she came in. A book lay closed on the armrest, his glasses balanced on top. He looked up, expectant, then paused.

"You're late," he said, not unkindly.

Mira slipped off her shoes and set her bag down. "Yes."

He frowned at the flatness of it, the lack of apology or excuse. She sat beside him, close enough to share the warmth of his body, but her stillness felt different, like someone standing in a doorway not yet committed to entering.

"Rough night?" he asked.

Her eyes lingered on the slow rise and fall of his chest, the way his breath moved under his shirt. Lawful, patterned, inevitable. But now she saw more. Beneath the machinery ran the gravity she had touched in the lab — a current so steady she could hardly believe she had missed it before.

She wanted to tell him, but words felt too brittle. Gloss could not carry what she had seen.

"Strange night," she said instead.

He studied her a moment longer, then gave a small smile. "That's your favorite word lately."

Mira tried to smile back, but it came out thin. She leaned her head against his shoulder. His warmth met her, human, anchoring. She let herself rest there, eyes closing.

For a moment she could almost forget the double vision: the dream world humming along, the substratum pulsing beneath it.

But she couldn't unsee. Every glance, every silence was layered now.

"You feel far away," James murmured.

"I'm here," she said softly. And it was true. But also not the whole truth.

He wrapped an arm around her anyway, pulling her in. She let him. The gesture was both pattern — attachment reflex, muscle and habit — and something larger, something that refused to collapse into explanation.

For a while they sat like that, the ordinary world moving around them: the hum of the refrigerator, the clock's soft tick, the city's muted breath through the window. Mira felt both comforted and estranged. It was all dream, but it was the dream she had to live in.

She opened her eyes and whispered, almost to herself, "This is the hard part."

James tilted his head. "What is?"

She shook her head, unwilling to drag him into a truth he had no way to hold. "Nothing. Just tired."

Later, when he had fallen asleep with the lamp still on, she lay awake beside him, watching his face in the glow. Ratios, reflexes, inevitability. And also — belonging. Love as gravity. Both at once.

Navigating the dream would not be easy. But she knew now that the dream was not all there was.

Among Others

The campus pulsed with its usual rhythms. Students crossed the quad in clumps, voices rising and falling in practiced cadences. A professor strode past with papers under his arm. A gardener bent to trim hedges, humming under his breath.

Mira moved through it slowly, hands buried in her coat pockets. Everything was ordinary. And everything was not.

The gloss still did its work — her mind labeled faces, sorted voices, smoothed the raw edges of motion. *Student. Teacher. Stranger.* A mercy. Without it the world would be unbearable.

But beneath the gloss the substratum pressed forward, insistent. She saw footsteps syncing unconsciously as groups formed, laughter falling in patterned bursts of call and response. She saw micro-hesitations, glances, hand movements — all lawful, all choreographed.

She had watched this before with the visor. Now she watched it without one. The vision no longer left her.

A pair of friends walked past, one speaking quickly, the other nodding in rhythm. She caught almost none of the words. What reached her was the engine beneath: one voice straining for reassurance, the other supplying it like oxygen. Need and answer. Inhale and exhale.

A pang caught in her chest. The dream world was necessary, but thin. How long could she live in it, knowing what lay beneath?

"Mira?"

She turned. One of her graduate students, tall, unkempt hair falling across his eyes, waved shyly. "I just wanted to say — the seminar last week… it really clicked for me. Thank you."

She opened her mouth, but the words tangled. His face was earnest, leaning on her acknowledgment. She saw the machinery of respect, the hunger for validation. And yet — there was warmth. Real warmth.

She managed a smile. "I'm glad it helped."

His face lit up. He thanked her again and jogged off.

Mira stood still, heart unsteady. The dream was fragile, but perhaps fragility itself was lawful. Gloss wasn't something to despise. It was something to tend — gently, like a fire sheltered from the wind.

She turned from the fountain and walked on.

Ana Alone

Ana hadn't slept well in days. Every time she closed her eyes the visor returned — not just the geometry, not just the ratios, but the hollow thrum of nothing beneath it all.

At first she resisted. She tried to distract herself with small routines: coffee brewed and left cooling, emails answered with half-thought replies, shows streaming in endless loops. None of it held. The void seeped through anyway. Every laugh track sounded like static. Every headline like noise. Even her own reflection in the bathroom mirror looked like scaffolding stretched over empty space.

She sat at her kitchen table, staring at an untouched mug.

Mira had called the experience beautiful. Love, she'd said. Wholeness. Ana almost envied her for that trick — envied the ability to cover the void with a word soft enough to live inside. But envy collapsed quickly into scorn. Love was just another label, another gloss Mira hadn't burned away.

The visor had stripped Ana clean. What remained wasn't tragic or heroic. It was machinery grinding on machinery. And that, she told herself, was the truth.

She whispered into the silence: "Meaning is anesthesia."

The phrase had been circling since the visor, and now, spoken aloud, it landed like a diagnosis. "It numbs you. The visor takes the painkiller away. No wonder people panic."

Her fingers tightened around the mug. If the world was void, then the sane response wasn't apathy — it was use. Pattern existed, and pattern could be bent. Maybe nothing mattered, but advantage did. To do nothing was to drown. To use was to stay afloat.

She flipped open her notebook. The pen moved quickly, steadying her with each line. Not theories. Not philosophy. Applications.

Interrogations. Negotiations. Elections. Markets.

Each word landed with weight. Each scenario offered leverage. She could almost feel her pulse slow, her breath find rhythm again. Utility was the thread she had left.

She closed the notebook and sat back. Mira had found her thread in love. Ana had found hers in use. Both were ways of surviving.

But she knew which one the world would pay for.

Ana with the Funders

The glass conference room was cold, sterile. She had sat here once with Mira, but now she was alone. Her notebook rested on the table, closed but heavy with diagrams and notes. She could almost feel the pulse of the words inside: meaning is anesthesia.

The lawyer entered first, his smile a blade thin enough to pass for polite. Behind him came the woman with her calm mask, and the two suited men whose eyes measured value the way brokers read tickers. They took their seats without preamble.

Ana met their gaze. "You want to know what it can do."

The lawyer gestured with two fingers. "Tell us."

She leaned forward, voice stripped clean of ornament. "The visor doesn't reveal truth. It subtracts story. What's left are signals — the body's unconscious math. Breath, cadence, hesitation. You've always guessed at them. The visor simply refuses to let you look away."

One of the men's lips curved. "Interrogation?"

"Efficient," Ana said. "No force required. Priors expose themselves. The body betrays the mind every time."

The woman's voice cut in, calm but edged. "Politics?"

Ana allowed herself a thin smile that never reached her eyes. "Politics is choreography. Cadence, repetition, symbol.

Feed the visor a speech and it will show you where the crowd's pulse will sync, which phrase will ignite, which image collapses resistance."

The second man leaned back, pleased. "As inevitable as you said."

Ana's hand tightened on her notebook. Mira's disapproval echoed in memory. But inevitability was the truth. The visor had stripped her illusions as ruthlessly as it stripped gloss from pattern.

"I'll give you a caveat," she said. Her voice hardened. "The visor doesn't only expose others. It exposes you. Push it too far, and your story unravels. Meaning thins. Law, morality, even love — illusions you rely on — become transparent. Fragile."

The lawyer tilted his head. "And yet you're here."

Ana shrugged, the motion precise. "Because illusions are anesthesia. They numb. The visor removes the drug. Most panic. I didn't. I adapted. That's why you want me."

The silence that followed wasn't resistance but calculation. They weren't deterred; they were mapping boundaries.

Finally the woman spoke, her calm sharpened into decision. "Then the question isn't if, but how — how to use it without unraveling the fabric we depend on."

Ana nodded. "Exactly."

The lawyer's smile returned, smooth as glass. "Then you'll be the one we trust with the first deployment."

A sting ran through her chest — betrayal of Mira, betrayal of herself — but she smothered it. This was survival. If the world was void, use was the only thread worth holding.

She closed the notebook with a deliberate snap. "Tell me what you need."

The Break-In

The lab was too still.

Mira stood by the bench, the visor humming faintly in its dock. She should have felt triumphant, even grateful, after what it had shown her. Instead she felt watched. Not by cameras or guards, but by the silence itself.

The funders hadn't called in days. No follow-ups, no questions, not even the perfunctory check-ins that once arrived with unnerving punctuality. Their absence was louder than their presence, like a breath held too long.

She sent a message to Ana. No reply. Another, hours later. Still nothing.

Ana's silence was worse than the funders'. It wasn't accidental. It was deliberate, chosen.

Mira walked the length of the lab, fingertips trailing along the stool, the whiteboard, the cabinets. Everything felt provisional, as though the walls themselves were waiting for permission to dissolve. Even the hum of the coolant lines carried a new edge, like a whisper cut short.

At night James noticed it too. "You've been jumpy," he said, watching her pace the apartment. "Like you're waiting for bad news."

She wanted to tell him it wasn't news she feared, but the lack of it. The stillness before a verdict. Decisions happening just beyond her reach, in rooms she wasn't invited to.

Instead she said, "It's nothing."

But it wasn't nothing. Every time she looked at the visor's cradle, its faint pulse seemed less like light and more like a beacon. A target. The thought returned, cold and certain: They're coming.

Mira knew something was wrong the moment her badge clicked green.

The door swung too easily, no resistance in the latch. Inside, the lab didn't smell like itself. No faint trace of solder, no sharp tang of ethanol. Just the sterile bite of disinfectant, as if the room had been erased.

She stopped short. The bench gleamed like it had never been used. The whiteboard was scrubbed to a blank shine. Even the fern was gone.

Her eyes leapt to the console. The cradle sat in its usual place, but it was empty.

She stood frozen, breath lodged in her throat. For a moment she almost expected the visor to reveal itself again, as if it had only been misplaced. But the void in the cradle remained, blunt and final.

On the console lay a single sheet of paper, block letters stamped across it:

PROPERTY OF STATE

Mira's hand shook as she picked it up. Her mind flinched toward explanations — relocation order, safety audit, anything. But the page was too stark. Too certain.

The anger came first. She slammed the paper against the bench, the crack echoing in the hollow room. Then grief followed, sudden and heavy, pulling her to the nearest stool.

The visor wasn't just a device. It was the mirror she had looked into, the thing that had shown her both terror and grace. Now it was gone.

She pressed her hands to her face. The silence pressed back.

Later, walking home, the world blurred into one long corridor. Cars passed, voices carried, but nothing registered. She could only see the empty cradle.

James asked her that evening why she was quiet. She almost told him everything. Instead, she said, "They've taken it."

He frowned. "Who?"

She shook her head, unable to give the answer aloud.

The page with its stamped words burned in her memory. PROPERTY OF STATE

The world had claimed what it did not understand.

James touched her arm, tentative, grounding. "Whatever it is, you're not alone."

She wanted to believe him. But the hollow inside her answered back: you are.

That night she couldn't sleep. She lay awake staring at the ceiling, her mind replaying the last few weeks like a cruel proof: the conference rooms, the laughter of the funders, Ana's silence. She had seen it coming, in the quiet, in the pauses. And she had done nothing.

Now it was out there. Not just in a vault. In motion.

Her stomach clenched as the thought unfolded: she had introduced a contagion of subtraction — a device that could strip the gloss from anyone, anywhere. A mirror that didn't just reflect but dissolved.

What if it spread too far? What if it made its way into interrogation rooms, campaign halls, classrooms? She could see it: the visor pulling patterns out of children, lovers, citizens, until the dream itself unraveled.

She pressed her palms over her eyes. It was unbearable, and yet she couldn't stop seeing it.

A sharper thought stabbed through: I should have protected it. I should have known they would come. She had spent years defending her work against skeptics, but she had never defended it against desire. Against power.

She sat up in bed, breath ragged. What was discovery worth, if it opened the door to this?

James stirred beside her. "Mira?"

"I'm fine," she whispered. But the words felt poisonous.

In the silence that followed, she realized the truth: her fear wasn't just for the visor's misuse. It was that she had been the one to place it in their reach.

She had built the key. And now the lock was gone.

Deployment

The room was windowless, painted in the same washed gray

as every government office Ana had ever seen. A table, two chairs, a pitcher of water. One way in, no way out.

The man across from her was thirty, maybe younger. Shaken but defiant. His wrists twitched against the cuffs, tiny betrayals of tension masquerading as control.

Ana lowered the visor onto her temples. The electrodes hummed.

At once, the man's defiance fractured. Not because he changed, but because the gloss dropped away. His breathing came in staccato bursts. His jaw locked, released, locked again. His voice — when he finally spoke — carried the same wobble she had heard in every nervous witness. Nothing mystical. Nothing hidden. Just signal.

Ana leaned forward. "Where were you the night of the fire?"

"I told you," he said, sharper than necessary. "Home."

The visor stripped the word, left the machinery. His shoulders tensed a fraction of a second before he spoke. His eyes darted right — fabrication hemisphere. A cough followed half a beat later — self-soothing reflex.

"Not home," Ana said flatly. "Try again."

The man's composure faltered. His lips parted, then shut. A tremor passed through his hands. The visor didn't expose guilt. It exposed fear's predictability, truth's erosion under pressure.

Ten minutes later he was broken open, the story spilling out in jagged fragments. He wasn't the arsonist, but he had known who was. He had been there. He had run.

The agents outside the door looked pleased. One gave Ana a nod, as if to say, efficient. Clean.

She pulled the visor off. The room returned to ordinary light, the man's sobs echoing against the walls.

For a moment, she felt nothing. Just pattern confirming itself, the lawfulness she had already accepted. But Mira's words nagged her like a splinter: Love remains.

Ana looked at the man and saw only machinery unraveling. No thread, no gravity, no wholeness — only a void.

She shoved the thought down hard, as if denying it could make it less true.

She stood, leaving the man to the guards.

In the corridor, the lawyer was waiting, smile thin as ever. "Exactly as promised," he said. "We'll want more of this."

Ana nodded, but her hands shook as she adjusted her coat. The tremor didn't feel like nerves. For the first time she noticed the air in the hallway carried no warmth.

The visor worked. And in its success, something in her thinned a little further.

Choreography

The auditorium smelled of stale coffee and stage lights. A senator stood at the podium, rehearsing the stump speech that would roll out next week. Staffers clustered at the back with clipboards, waiting for the right phrases to land.

Ana sat in the front row, visor snug against her temples.

The words came, smooth and practiced. But the visor

refused the gloss. Each sentence broke down into currents of rhythm and gesture. The rise of the senator's hand, the drop of a syllable, the pause before the applause line — all equations, all predictable.

Ana adjusted the dial. Instantly, the room rewrote itself. She saw where the cadence stumbled, where the metaphors failed to sync, where the crowd would resist. Even without a crowd present, the priors showed themselves. The body rehearsed not just for itself but for the thousands it expected.

"Stop," Ana said.

The senator froze, startled.

"Your second paragraph. The line about jobs. Cut it. Replace with something local, something that mirrors their pride. Then lift your pitch half a step. Hold the pause. They'll sync with you whether they want to or not."

He hesitated. "That precise?"

Ana almost laughed. "It isn't precision. It's law. You only think you're persuading them. In reality, you're riding machinery that was already there."

He adjusted the line, read again. The visor lit with harmony: cadence aligned, posture eased, the probability of applause surged.

Ana removed the visor. "Better."

The staffers clapped politely, relief mixed with unease.

The senator stepped down, patting her shoulder. "You'll make me unstoppable."

Ana forced a smile. But inside, a fissure widened. The

visor had just shown her the future applause like a weather forecast — percentages, inevitabilities. The crowd would clap not because of conviction but because their reflexes had been tuned like strings.

Mira had once seen tenderness in inevitability, the law as something that bound without cruelty. Ana saw only choreography, hollowed out.

Her stomach tightened. She slipped the visor into its case, palms slick with sweat.

Meaning is anesthesia, she reminded herself. But the words no longer numbed.

Utility was survival. And yet with every deployment, survival shrank to a narrower shape.

Fracture

The meeting was a closed-door negotiation, higher stakes than anything Ana had yet touched. Senior officials from defense, commerce, and intelligence crowded the table, aides lined up against the walls with tablets glowing. The agenda: budget allocations — billions to be carved up under the banner of "national security."

Ana sat near the end, visor snug, a silent observer.

For weeks she had told herself the same thing: utility is survival. The world didn't care if you loved it. It cared if you were useful. And she would be indispensable — the one who could look through the gloss, strip every mask, see the leverage no one else could. That was strength. That was safety.

The speeches began. On the surface: measured, polite. Through the visor: rancid.

Each word of "stability" pulsed with fear. Each invocation of "collaboration" trembled with rivalry. The defense official's fists clenched under the table every time "budget cuts" were mentioned. The commerce secretary's pitch dropped half a step whenever profit hid behind patriotism. The intelligence chief's smile stretched too wide, contempt bleeding through the feigned courtesy.

Concealment wasn't the exception; it was the law of the room.

At first, Ana rode the patterns like a wave. Yes. This is what they need me for. She tracked every falsehood, every fracture, mapping their weakness with clinical precision.

But the patterns multiplied. Every hesitation demanded her attention. Every false smile became unbearable. She could hear their lies even in their silences, see the betrayals twitching in their muscles before words arrived.

Her stomach twisted. She swallowed hard, fingers tightening against the console. Control yourself.

Then a cough — just a junior aide clearing his throat after his superior misspoke — hit her like a thunderclap. The deceit wasn't occasional. It was everywhere, the very medium the meeting breathed.

Her chest clenched. The visor hummed mercilessly, showing her what she had once suspected but never truly felt: society itself ran on concealment.

She ripped the visor off, shoved back her chair, and stumbled into the corridor. A trash can stood by the wall. She bent over and vomited, bitter acid scraping her throat, tears burning her eyes. It felt like her body was expelling the lies she could no longer digest.

The world tilted. She pressed a hand to the cold plaster, gasping, trying to anchor herself. This wasn't just nausea. It was recognition. Beneath the choreography, there was no bedrock. Only projection against projection, lies feeding on lies. Mira had called the patterns beautiful. To Ana they tasted like bile.

Her mantra rang hollow: utility is survival. It no longer steadied her. It mocked her. Because if everything was utility, then nothing had meaning — and meaning was what her body was begging for.

She stumbled into the restroom, rinsed her mouth, splashed cold water onto her face. The fluorescent light showed her reflection pale and streaked, veins standing out at her temples. Indispensable? She looked like a tool already spent.

When she returned to the hall, the lawyer was waiting. His smile was intact, but his eyes scanned her like a ledger.

"You'll adapt," he murmured.

Ana forced a nod. "Of course."

But the air had shifted. One of the officials leaned toward a colleague, hand cupped to his mouth. Another's gaze lingered on her trembling hand as she set her notebook down. A faint shake of the head — the kind reserved for equipment starting to fail. The room had already begun recalculating without her.

Ana lowered her eyes, pretending to take notes. Inside, her chest hollowed. For weeks she had believed she was the one strong enough to wield the visor. But strength had curdled into fracture, and the room had seen it.

For the first time, she felt what they saw: not asset, not oracle. Just another tool breaking down.

The Return

Mira still passed the lab some evenings on her way out of the building. The door was padlocked, the placard gone, but habit drew her down the corridor like a ghost retracing old steps.

Tonight, the lock hung loose. The door stood ajar.

Inside, the lab was bare as before. But a figure sat hunched on the stool by the console, head in her hands.

Ana.

Her hair was unkempt, her blazer wrinkled, eyes sunk into bruised hollows. The sharpness that had once bristled in every gesture was gone. She looked smaller, as though something inside her had been hollowed out.

Mira stepped in, the door clicking shut behind her.

Ana lifted her head slowly. She tried to summon defiance, but the words broke into a brittle laugh. "They used me," she said. Her voice was hoarse, stripped of its edge. "For a while I thought I was indispensable. Then I cracked. And they dropped me like a bad tool."

Mira said nothing.

Ana's eyes burned. "You warned me. I told myself you were weak, sentimental. But the visor — " Her voice trembled. "It ate through me. Every room, every person… nothing but lies stacked on lies. They wanted me to wield it, to turn it into leverage. I thought I could live with that. I thought I could use it."

Her hands clenched into fists. "But there's no using it. It uses you. Until you're nothing. I vomited in a hallway while they whispered about whether I was 'fit for service.' They were right. I wasn't."

Silence settled heavy in the stripped room.

Mira crossed the room, her hand brushing the cool bench. The cradle sat empty, but the absence hummed between them.

"You saw the void," she said softly.

Ana gave a broken nod. "And nothing beyond it."

Mira's voice was steady. "The void is real. But it isn't the whole."

Ana barked a laugh that tipped into something like a sob. "It was stripping me alive. Every smile, every word, every touch — all machinery. I thought I could stomach it, but it made me sick. Literally sick. I came out ruined."

Mira lowered herself onto the opposite stool. She didn't argue. She didn't console. She simply looked at Ana with the same calm that had steadied her through her own abyss.

Ana shook her head, angry tears spilling. "I don't

understand how you bore it. How you looked into that thing and came out… softer. Stronger."

Mira's lips curved faintly, not in triumph but in recognition.

"You stopped too soon," she said.

Ana stared at her, breathing unevenly.

They sat in the gutted lab, two women facing each other across the empty bench, the absence of the visor more eloquent than its presence had ever been.

Ana broke the silence at last, voice raw. "I was wrong." She looked up, eyes wet but unguarded. "About you. About me. About everything."

Mira didn't move to close the distance. She only let the words settle, real as the blank walls around them.

Ana's shoulders shook once, then stilled. "What do I do now?"

Mira drew a slow breath.

"Live in the dream," she said quietly. "See through it when you can. And when you can't — remember it isn't yours alone to carry."

Ana closed her eyes, tears running freely now. She didn't argue. She didn't ask again.

For a long time they sat in the empty room, the hum of absence holding them both.

The Burial

It surfaced on page seventeen of a government bulletin,

buried between appropriations tables and an announcement about new postal facilities.

Matter of record: *Applied Perception Research Initiative suspended indefinitely. All materials placed under classified review. Further dissemination prohibited.*

No mention of NOEMA. No mention of the visor. Just an anemic phrase — *applied perception research* — reducing years of work to a line item, then entombing it.

Mira read the paragraph twice, then folded the paper. It was what she had expected. Still, the bluntness of it made her throat tighten.

Later that evening she searched the news, but found nothing. A few rumors in the trade blogs about "experimental cognition projects" being shelved, whispers about psychological risk. But no one outside the circle would ever know.

The State had buried it cleanly, as it had buried so many other dangerous discoveries.

Only this one wasn't dangerous in the usual way. Not a missile whose trajectory could be tracked. Not a pathogen multiplying in bloodstreams. No explosive yield, no visible casualties.

Its hazard was subtler. More corrosive.

The visor was a solvent poured over the fabric of human life. It stripped away the fictions people required to stand upright: patriotism, romance, law, even the fragile story of self. With it, loyalty curdled into reflex, justice into probability, love into a spasm of muscle and light.

Every story dissolved, leaving only machinery.

Too dangerous to use, because no institution built on belief could survive it. Courts depended on witnesses swearing to truth, churches on the authority of mystery, governments on the spectacle of trust. Even families — even the whispered stories parents told their children at night — would collapse if every gesture were revealed as patterned inevitability.

And markets? The most invisible fiction of all. Credit, debt, confidence — ghosts pretending to be solid. If enough eyes saw through the gloss, the entire edifice would fold like paper in water.

And yet it was too true to destroy. Once seen, it could not be unseen. The reports were filed. The data copied. The equations already scattered across servers, waiting. To smash the visor itself was nothing; its insight had already slipped free, uncontainable.

So the State did the only thing it could: it buried it. Stamped the papers, locked the prototypes in a vault, sealed the files behind firewalls and classification codes. A line of bureaucratic ink masquerading as control.

Not erased — never erased — only hidden.

A hum silenced in the open world, but still vibrating beneath it, waiting for the next pair of eyes bold — or foolish — enough to look.

Mira sat at her kitchen table, the folded paper before her, the lamp pooling light across the page. James moved quietly in the background, washing dishes, humming faintly to himself.

The world staggered on.

CUT FROM THE SAME CLOTH

The Checklist

By the time he reached the bottom of the file, he already knew how it would end.

The claim involved a house fire in a quiet subdivision outside Sacramento. No injuries. Moderate damage. The adjuster's photos showed the same familiar details: blackened studs, a warped refrigerator door, a collapsed section of roof where the heat had pooled. The cause was listed as electrical, which almost always meant space heater, which almost always meant extension cord.

He checked the boxes in the order he'd learned to check them. Property type. Weather conditions. Occupancy status. Time of day. He did this carefully, not because it was difficult, but because small errors had a way of compounding later. Somewhere downstream, numbers would be tallied, premiums adjusted, assumptions revised. It wasn't dramatic work, but it was expensive when done poorly.

At the bottom of the page, he paused.

The loss profile was clean. Too clean. It matched the last three he'd reviewed almost exactly — not identical, but close enough that he felt the faint irritation he'd learned to associate with repetition. He scrolled back up and compared them side by side.

Different neighborhoods. Different families. Same sequence of events.

He told himself it was coincidence. Or volume. Or the simple fact that people tended to live the same lives in the same kinds of houses, with the same kinds of habits. That was, after all, the premise of the entire industry.

Still, before closing the file, he highlighted one line and made a note in the margin:

Loss progression unusually consistent across recent claims.

It wasn't an escalation. Just a flag. The kind of thing that disappeared into quarterly reviews and came back months later, stripped of its context.

The office around him moved at its usual low hum. Phones rang and were answered politely. Someone laughed too loudly at a desk nearby and then stopped. The air-conditioning cycled on and off. On a screen mounted above the break room, a news anchor spoke with controlled excitement about continued developments and pending confirmation.

He didn't look up.

At lunch, he ate a sandwich at his desk and reviewed two more claims. A multi-car accident during a sudden rainstorm. A burst pipe in a vacant commercial building. Different events, same outcome curves. The language varied slightly — unexpected, unfortunate, hard to predict — but the numbers behaved themselves.

They always did.

A coworker leaned over the low divider separating their

desks.

"Did you see the footage?" she asked.

"Of what?"

She raised her eyebrows. "The thing. The big thing."

He shook his head. "I've been buried."

"Well," she said, smiling in a way that suggested both excitement and nerves, "apparently everyone's losing their minds."

"About time," he said, and meant it kindly.

She laughed and wandered off.

That afternoon, he ran a simple comparison — nothing fancy, just a cross-check against historical data. Fires like this had happened before. Thousands of times. Decades' worth. The curve tightened as expected. No surprises. No outliers. The model absorbed the new data without complaint.

That should have been the end of it.

But as he closed the program, he noticed something that made him sit back in his chair. It wasn't that the claims were similar. It was how few variations there actually were once you stripped away the surface details.

He opened an older file at random. Same pattern. Another. Same.

The irritation returned, sharper now — not curiosity, exactly, but the discomfort of something refusing to resolve. He saved a copy of the comparison to a personal folder, one he used rarely and labeled plainly: *Review*.

At home that evening, his partner had the news on while

they cooked. Analysts debated implications. Religious leaders offered cautious statements. Someone on the screen used the word unprecedented three times in a single sentence.

"Do you think this changes anything?" she asked, handing him a knife.

He shrugged. "Insurance will go up," he said.

She laughed, then stopped. "You're impossible."

"Occupational hazard."

Later, lying in bed, he thought again about the claims — not the damage, but the way the outcomes had folded so neatly into one another, as if there had only ever been a small number of ways for things to go wrong.

It wasn't troubling. Not yet.

Just narrower than he'd expected.

Actuarial Weather

The next morning brought rain.

It wasn't heavy, just steady enough to slow traffic and lengthen commute times. By the time he reached the office, his shoes were damp and his jacket smelled faintly of wool and exhaust. He hung it on the back of his chair and logged in, already anticipating the day's queue.

Weather always did this. A shift in conditions, and the claims followed like obedient children.

The first file involved a three-car collision on an overpass. No fatalities. One broken wrist. The report used the familiar language — *slick pavement, reduced visibility, failure to maintain distance.* He checked the boxes without resistance, then moved on.

The second was similar. Different city. Same hour of the morning. Same phrasing, almost word for word.

By the fourth, he stopped reading the narrative altogether and went straight to the summary fields. The numbers told the story more efficiently. Speeds, angles, points of impact. When he finished, he leaned back and stared at the ceiling tiles, which had been replaced the year before but still showed faint outlines of old water stains.

He opened the comparison tool again.

This time, he didn't bother adjusting the parameters. He knew what he would see. The curves overlapped neatly, the margins collapsing toward a center he could almost predict now. The data didn't resist. It rarely did.

Insurance was often described as a way of managing uncertainty, but that wasn't quite right. Most of the uncertainty had already been wrung out of things long before the claims reached his desk. What remained was variation in detail, not outcome.

A colleague from two desks over wheeled her chair closer.

"You seeing this too?" she asked, tapping her screen.

"Seeing what?"

She frowned. "It's like everyone learned how to crash the same way."

He smiled. "They probably did."

She laughed, then shook her head. "Feels wrong, doesn't

it? Like the universe is cutting corners."

"Efficiency," he said. "Hard to argue with."

She rolled her eyes and spun back toward her desk.

Midmorning, a notification popped up on his screen announcing an internal briefing later that week: *Anticipated Behavioral Impacts – External Events.* The subject line didn't say much, but the subtext was obvious. Everyone was preparing for something they couldn't model yet.

At lunch, the cafeteria buzzed louder than usual. Phones were out. Conversations overlapped. Someone had pulled up a live feed and turned the volume too high.

He ate slowly, listening without fully attending. The speculation had taken on a fevered quality. People talked about panic buying, mass migration, market collapse. Someone mentioned looting. Another mentioned awakening. The words didn't line up, but the emotional charge did.

When he returned to his desk, there were six new claims waiting.

A warehouse fire. A flooded basement. A slip-and-fall in a grocery store. Different categories, different policy types. He worked through them methodically, feeling the now-familiar tightening when the outcomes began to align.

At one point, he caught himself guessing the resolution before he reached the end of the report. He was right more often than not.

That bothered him.

Not because it felt ominous, but because it felt final. As if the work had become less about learning and more about confirmation. He wasn't sure when that shift had happened, only that it had.

In the late afternoon, he pulled up a decade-old dataset, something he rarely did. The files loaded slowly, the interface clunkier, the notes written in a different corporate voice. He chose a random year and ran the same basic comparisons.

The pattern tightened again.

He sat with it longer this time, hands folded loosely in his lap. The room around him faded — the hum of the lights, the distant ring of a phone, the low murmur of voices drifting from a conference room down the hall.

It occurred to him, not for the first time, that the language used to describe these events — *accident, incident, unexpected* — was misleading. Not wrong, exactly. Just… generous.

At home that evening, his partner was restless. She paced between the kitchen and the living room, phone in hand, refreshing feeds he didn't ask about.

"They're saying people are already pulling their kids out of school," she said.

"Because of tomorrow?"

"Because of everything."

He nodded and chopped vegetables more carefully than necessary.

"Doesn't it feel like we're all waiting for something?" she asked.

"Yes," he said. "We usually are."

She studied him for a moment. "You don't sound scared."

"I'm not," he said, then paused. "I don't think fear would help."

Later, as they sat on the couch with the lights dimmed, a commentator on the screen spoke urgently about preparedness and resilience. The words washed over him. He was thinking instead about the warehouse fire, about how the report had used the phrase rapid escalation to describe something that followed a sequence he could now recite from memory.

When he went to bed, he opened his laptop one last time and pulled up the folder labeled Review. He added a new file, then another. He didn't rename them. Just let them sit there, accumulating.

Before closing the lid, he typed a short note to himself:

Variation decreases under pressure.

He stared at the sentence, then deleted it.

He replaced it with something safer:

Patterns stable across stress conditions.

That would do.

Outside, the rain had stopped. The street was quiet, reflective, the wet pavement catching light from the lamps in familiar, orderly ways.

He slept more deeply than he had the night before.

Loss Ratios

By midweek, the office had taken on a strange, anticipatory

quiet.

People still worked. Phones still rang. Emails still arrived in steady waves. But beneath it all ran a current of distraction, as if everyone were waiting for an announcement they didn't quite trust would come. Conversations broke off mid-sentence. Screens were checked more often than necessary.

He noticed this the way he noticed most things lately — without commentary.

His inbox was heavier than usual. Not with new claims, exactly, but with revised projections, internal notes, reminders to "document assumptions clearly." The language had shifted. Where before there had been confidence in margins and buffers, there was now caution. Conditional phrasing. Footnotes multiplying like spores.

Insurance did not like uncertainty it couldn't price.

The morning's work involved compiling a summary for a quarterly review — loss ratios across several regions, adjusted for recent events. It was the kind of task that usually bored him. This time, it held his attention.

The ratios were compressing.

Not dramatically. Nothing that would justify a meeting. But enough that he found himself rechecking the formulas, then checking them again. The expected spread had narrowed. Risk was behaving itself.

He thought, briefly, of the phrase *regression to the mean*, then dismissed it. That implied deviation first. What he was seeing felt more like inevitability asserting itself early.

A message popped up from his supervisor asking whether he'd noticed anything unusual.

He stared at the question longer than necessary.

Unusual was a strong word. Everything fit. That was the problem.

He typed a careful reply:

No significant anomalies. Some convergence in outcomes, but within historical precedent.

He sent it and felt a small, familiar relief.

Late in the morning, a fire alarm went off somewhere in the building — a false one, judging by the lack of urgency. People stood, waited, then sat back down when the announcement crackled over the intercom. Someone made a joke about drills and preparedness. Someone else mentioned timing.

He returned to his spreadsheet.

At lunch, he joined a few coworkers at a long table near the windows. The conversation drifted, as it had all week, toward speculation.

"They won't show us everything," one of them said.

"They can't," another replied. "Markets would panic."

"I heard they already have," someone else said, lowering their voice.

He listened, nodded when appropriate, but said little. He had learned that uncertainty made people narrate more loudly. Silence was often taken as dissent, but he didn't mind that.

"What do you think?" someone asked him finally.

He considered the question. "I think people will behave the way they usually do," he said.

There was a pause. A few puzzled looks.

"That's not very comforting," someone said.

He smiled apologetically. "It's not meant to be."

That afternoon, a new set of claims arrived flagged time-sensitive. Not catastrophic, just clustered — a rash of minor injuries, property damage tied to crowding, delays, miscommunications. The causes varied. The outcomes did not.

He worked through them steadily, feeling the now-familiar sense of compression. The same failure points. The same delays. The same attempts to assign blame after the fact.

At one point, he caught himself thinking: There are only so many ways this can go.

The thought startled him. Not because it felt profound, but because it felt obvious — as if he'd always known it and simply hadn't bothered to articulate it before.

He pushed the thought aside and kept working.

When he got home, his partner was on the phone with her sister. Her voice was tight, the way it got when she was trying to sound calm.

"Yes, I know," she said. "No, I don't think they'll shut everything down… Well, maybe temporarily."

She hung up and exhaled.

"Everyone's on edge," she said.

He nodded. "That happens when expectations widen."

She looked at him. "You always talk like that."

"Like what?"

"Like you're already on the other side of things."

He didn't have an answer for that. He set his bag down and went to the kitchen, rinsed his hands, and began setting the table. The ritual steadied him.

That night, the news finally announced a date.

The reveal would happen soon. A controlled environment. Limited access. Live coverage with a delay. The anchors spoke in solemn tones, careful not to speculate too much while doing exactly that.

His partner watched intently. He watched her.

"What if everything changes?" she asked.

He thought of the spreadsheets, the narrowing curves, the way loss ratios settled into place no matter how chaotic the event that produced them.

"Some things will," he said. "Most things won't."

She shook her head, half-smiling. "You're impossible."

Later, alone at his desk, he opened the Review folder again. The files had accumulated quietly, a small archive of sameness. He didn't open them. He didn't need to.

Instead, he stared at the empty space between icons and wondered — briefly, without urgency — whether there was any reason to expect the universe to behave differently than people did.

The thought didn't frighten him.

If anything, it felt like a narrowing of responsibility.

He shut down the computer and turned off the light.

Compression

The office felt smaller as the date approached.

Not physically — the same rows of desks, the same neutral walls — but atmospherically, as if the range of possible conversations had narrowed. People spoke in lower voices. Meetings ran long and ended without conclusions. Everyone seemed to be waiting for permission to react.

He kept working.

The claims arriving now were subtly different. Not larger, not more severe — just closer together in time. Minor damages clustered around the same hours. The same locations appeared again and again. The same phrases repeated in reports written by different adjusters who had never met.

Failure to anticipate volume.

Insufficient guidance.

Unexpected congestion.

He marked them, tagged them, moved on.

Mid-morning, he received a request from another department asking for a quick synthesis — nothing formal, just an internal snapshot. *Are we seeing anything that might affect exposure?*

He considered the question carefully.

Exposure implied risk beyond tolerance. What he was seeing sat squarely inside tolerance, pressed firmly against its center. He typed a response that took longer than it should have.

Behavior remains consistent with prior large-scale events. No evidence of novel risk vectors.

He reread the sentence, then sent it.

A few minutes later, a reply came back: *That's… reassuring.*

He wasn't sure why.

At lunch, he walked outside instead of eating at his desk. The sky was clear, the air cool. A line had formed at the coffee shop across the street, longer than usual, people standing closer together than they normally would. He watched them shuffle forward, phones in hand, expressions alert but contained.

He had the passing thought — faint, almost impersonal — that if something went wrong right now, the outcomes would be predictable.

The thought no longer irritated him.

Back inside, his supervisor stopped by his desk.

"Everything good?"

"Yes."

"You're sure?"

He nodded. "As sure as I can be."

She lingered, then said, "It's strange, isn't it?"

"What is?"

"All of this."

He glanced at her, then at his screen. "Only if you expect it to be."

She frowned slightly, as if trying to parse that, then smiled and moved on.

That afternoon, he found himself skipping steps he no longer needed. Not recklessly — just efficiently. He knew where the reports would end before they did. The work felt less like analysis and more like recognition.

For the first time, he wondered whether this was what mastery looked like — not control, but familiarity taken so far it ceased to feel informative.

At home, his partner was restless again. She moved from room to room, adjusting things that didn't need adjusting.

"Everyone at work is distracted," she said. "No one can focus."

He nodded. "Focus usually returns once expectations settle."

She stopped and looked at him. "You really believe that, don't you?"

He thought about the way curves tightened, how variation collapsed once enough data was collected. "I think expectations create more noise than events," he said.

She sighed. "I wish I could see it that way."

That night, sleep came easily. When he dreamed, it was of diagrams without labels, shapes settling into place without resistance.

The morning of the reveal arrived quietly.

There were no sirens. No crowds outside his building. Just an unusual number of people already awake, already watching. He dressed, made coffee, checked his phone out of habit.

The coverage would begin mid-morning.

At work, screens were already on. Some people gathered near the break room. Others stayed at their desks, pretending not to care. He did both — he queued the stream in a small window at the corner of his monitor and returned to his work.

The first claim of the day involved a minor injury during a rush to evacuate a transit station the night before. No serious harm. The report ended with a familiar phrase: *Sequence escalated faster than anticipated.*

He highlighted it, then removed the highlight.

The feed in the corner of the screen shifted to a wide shot of a sealed chamber. Neutral lighting. No dramatic angles. The commentators spoke softly, filling the space with context and caveats.

He felt no anticipation.

If anything, he felt a curious sense of completion — as if something he'd been tracking unconsciously had finally reached its last data point.

He minimized the window and finished the report.

The Door

The chamber was smaller than he'd imagined.

Not cramped, exactly, but modest — functional in the way rooms were when no one wanted to impose a narrative on them. Smooth walls. Even lighting. No banners, no symbols. The kind of place designed to minimize interpretation.

He watched from his desk, the feed occupying a rectangle at the corner of his screen. Around him, the office had gone still. No phones rang. No one spoke. Even the air-conditioning seemed to pause between cycles.

A commentator murmured something about containment protocols. Another voice listed dimensions and materials. None of it mattered.

The camera shifted.

The door stood flush with the wall, its outline barely visible until a seam appeared, then widened. There was no dramatic sound — just a soft mechanical movement, deliberate and controlled.

For a moment, nothing happened.

Then they stepped forward.

They wore simple, close-fitting garments in muted tones, practical rather than ceremonial, and stood at roughly human height, differing only in the ordinary ways bodies do.

They were upright.

That was the first thing he noticed — not because it was surprising, but because it settled something immediately. Balance distributed over two legs. Weight adjusted subtly, the way people did when they were unsure of footing.

Their skin was pale. Not uniformly so, but lightly pigmented, almost translucent in places. Veins visible beneath the surface, faint and branching. Hair was sparse, fine, close to the scalp. Their faces resisted classification — familiar without being specific, as if features had been averaged rather than inherited.

One of them held their hands folded in front of their

body. Another let their arms hang at their sides, then shifted, mirroring the first. A third glanced downward briefly before looking up again, a gesture so small it would have been easy to miss.

He leaned closer to the screen.

They were still. Not rigid. Just waiting.

Someone near the microphone spoke — a greeting, carefully phrased. There was a pause, then a response through the translator. The cadence was halting, measured. Not alien in the way he'd once imagined. More like someone choosing words with care.

As the exchange continued, he found himself paying less attention to what was said and more to how they moved. The slight sway. The adjustment of stance. A sheen of moisture along the temple of the one closest to the camera.

Perspiration.

The realization arrived without ceremony.

They were nervous.

Not theatrically. Not in a way that demanded empathy. Just enough to register — the same bodily response he'd seen a thousand times in claims reports, in witness statements, in photographs taken moments after something irreversible had happened.

Around him, someone inhaled sharply. Someone else whispered, "They're just… like us."

He didn't disagree, but the phrase felt imprecise.

It wasn't that they were like *us*.

It was that they were like this.

Bounded. Upright. Subject to gravity and hesitation and the need to place one's hands somewhere when standing in front of an audience.

The camera angle changed, offering a wider view. The chamber looked smaller now, occupied by bodies that fit it almost too well. The commentators struggled to keep pace, their language searching for emphasis that never quite landed.

He glanced back at his screen — at the unfinished claim waiting for his attention. The words *sequence escalated faster than anticipated* stared back at him, suddenly stripped of drama.

There were only so many ways for things to unfold.

He felt no disappointment. No awe.

Just a quiet sense of confirmation, as if the last piece of data had finally arrived and behaved exactly as expected.

The feed continued. Questions were asked. Answers attempted. Somewhere in the building, someone began to cry.

He minimized the window.

For a long moment, he sat with his hands resting on the desk, fingers lightly touching, posture unconsciously mirroring what he'd just seen.

Then he returned to work.

Settlement

The reaction arrived before the meaning did.

Within hours, statements were issued. Clarifications followed clarifications. Markets dipped, then corrected themselves. Religious leaders revised sermons already written. Commentators searched for language that could carry the moment without sounding foolish once it settled.

People had prepared themselves for enormity. What they received felt smaller — not trivial, but contained. The initial awe thinned quickly, replaced by questions no one quite knew how to ask.

At work, the next day unfolded with surprising normalcy.

The inbox filled early. Claims tied indirectly to the event began appearing — crowd injuries, minor property damage, stress-related incidents, infrastructure strained by attention rather than use. Nothing catastrophic. Nothing unfamiliar.

He reviewed them steadily, noticing how quickly the language reverted to form. The same phrases. The same attempts to assign causality after the fact. The same insistence that this moment had been impossible to anticipate.

The numbers disagreed.

By midday, a brief internal memo circulated summarizing the firm's preliminary assessment. *No immediate deviation from projected exposure. Behavioral responses within modeled parameters.*

He read it once, then archived it.

At lunch, the cafeteria buzzed again, but the pitch had changed. The excitement was gone, replaced by something like recalibration. People argued about interpretations now — what it *meant*, what it *should have been*. A few seemed angry, though they couldn't quite say why.

He ate quietly and returned to his desk.

That afternoon, he closed several open loops — follow-ups he'd left pending, comparisons he no longer felt compelled to revisit. The *Review* folder remained untouched. There was nothing more to add.

At home, his partner was subdued. She sat on the couch with the television off, the room lit only by the late light coming through the windows.

"I don't know what I was expecting," she said finally.

She leaned her head against his shoulder. They stayed that way for a while, listening to the building settle — pipes ticking, a door closing somewhere down the hall.

He thought of the chamber. The posture. The nervousness that hadn't needed translation.

Later, as he washed the dishes, he caught his reflection in the darkened window — his stance relaxed, hands resting easily at his sides. The image reminded him, fleetingly, of the figures in the chamber, waiting.

He dried his hands and turned off the light.

There were only so many ways.

THE SMELL OF GREEN

Choosing

There was a girl once.

Her name was Anya. She lived down the street and always had a pink band-aid somewhere on her skin — elbow, wrist, the ridge of her shin. One spring afternoon, when Eliot was nine, she found him standing at the edge of his front yard, watching the other kids set up a basketball hoop in the cul-de-sac. She walked right up and said, "You're always looking, never playing."

He didn't know what to say, so he said nothing.

She pulled a leaf from the hedge, pushed it under his nose, and said, "Smell it. Smells like green." Then she ran off barefoot, laughing, before he could respond.

He remembered that for the rest of his life — not because it was important, but because nothing ever quite replaced it.

—

He watched a lot as a child. From windows, from the back seat of the car, from behind glowing glass. Watching was safe. Interacting, less so. Other kids were loud, physical, unpredictable. The digital world, by contrast, asked nothing he couldn't give. He could mute what annoyed him, rewind what confused him, skip what bored him. And over time, real life began to feel clumsy. Heavy. Too slow for his mind.

He still played outside sometimes — until fourth grade. He was fast, with good reflexes, and once blocked a taller boy's layup. They slapped his back and called him "E-Z." He didn't hate it. But he didn't miss it either once it was gone.

His mother said the school was changing. Getting too political. Too much focus on identity, too little on math and science. One day, after a tense parent meeting, she said she'd had enough. "You're smarter than all this. We'll do better at home."

Eliot didn't argue. He liked home.

He liked the way his room lit up when he asked it to. The way his tablet remembered where he left off. The way his games welcomed him like a hero returning from war. And most of all, he liked the forums — the message boards where other kids posted walkthroughs, jokes, and GIFs about their favorite worlds. No awkward small talk. No waiting your turn. Just pure, shared obsession.

At eleven, he joined a Minecraft modding group and published a custom expansion that got five thousand downloads in a week. His screen name, "HeliOs," started showing up in comment threads. Someone made him a logo. Someone else called him a prodigy. He copied that into his profile and stared at it often.

Outside, the world moved on. Anya stopped coming around. The boys down the street got taller and louder. The basketball hoop sagged. And Eliot stayed indoors, where the feedback was cleaner, the wins more obvious.

He didn't feel like he was missing anything. Not then. In fact, he felt like he was getting ahead.

Sometimes, though, before the screen pulled him in for the day, he would wander outside after breakfast — barefoot, holding a slice of toast, blinking into the sun.

The air felt different in the morning — not just cooler, but younger, like the day hadn't yet decided what it would become.

Eliot would just stand there sometimes, letting the sun warm his skin through his t-shirt, watching a snail make its slow pilgrimage along the brick border near the roses. He didn't think to name the feeling. It wasn't joy exactly. More like a quiet permission to belong to the world.

And then he'd hear the digital chime of an incoming chat message.

And just like that, the moment would evaporate.

—

By twelve, Eliot was already doing better than most kids his age — at least by the numbers.

He aced his online classes. Not just with good grades, but with glowing feedback. His logic skills tested high percentile. His essays were flagged for "voice maturity." His math instructor — a soft-voiced AI in the shape of an owl — once called him "exceptionally self-regulating." He clipped that phrase and saved it to his desktop.

He wasn't just smart. He was proficient. He completed modules early. Read white papers about probability theory. Dabbled in machine learning courses made for college students. And at night, he played.

Games were more than games. They were his country — a realm where fluency meant access, where skill earned admiration. In a PvP shooter, he climbed the ranks so fast that strangers asked to team up with him. His screen name became a kind of shield — no one knew he was a quiet twelve-year-old in gym shorts, eating yogurt tubes in a dark room. They just knew he was good.

That year, he minted his first crypto token. A tutorial showed him how to script it, assign value, simulate scarcity. He sold it on a digital marketplace and made six hundred dollars in three days. His parents were baffled, impressed, slightly concerned. They praised him — but cautiously. They still hoped he'd make "real" friends.

He didn't see the need.

The real turning came one afternoon in early summer, right around the end of seventh grade.

He was coding a texture pack for a medieval-style building sim — tuning the look of rust on chainmail — when a text popped up on his family's shared tablet. A boy named Marcus, who lived two doors down, was having a birthday thing at the park. Pickup soccer, burgers, music. *"Bring a friend,"* the message said. *"2PM. Come chill with us."*

Eliot read it twice. Then looked at the clock. 1:43.

He stood up. Walked to the window. The sky was bright — too bright — and the trees were loud with wind. He pictured Marcus and the others kicking a ball, shouting, laughing. Getting dirty. Elbows, teasing, someone tripping, someone yelling "Goal!"

He felt something tighten in his chest.

Then he sat down. Slipped his headphones back on. Pulled the texture window back up. Clicked open a new chat with a gamer in Norway who had been giving him tips on surface mapping.

"I don't really like those kids," he muttered to no one. "Their games are stupid."

He didn't say it with bitterness. Just with finality.

Like a boy closing a book and placing it on a shelf he'd never reach for again.

Substitution

By the time Eliot turned fifteen, the world had become very smart — and he, very still.

AI had bloomed like mold across every surface of life: in the tools people used, in the apps they spoke through, in the soft glow of virtual faces that never misunderstood. Everything was smoother now. The interfaces had softened. The delays were gone. Feedback came in real time, perfectly tuned. And Eliot — already online, already leaning inward — barely noticed the transition.

He was thriving, according to most metrics. He'd passed his courses early, launched a few small crypto projects, even received a certificate of "Innovation & Design" from a virtual mentor network partnered with Stanford's AI lab. His screen name, *HeliOs*, still carried weight in modding forums. A gaming podcast had once called him "a quiet legend of the early decade."

And yet his room smelled faintly of dust and half-life — discarded wrappers, stale energy drink, the sweet metal scent of overheated hardware. The blinds hadn't been opened in weeks. Outside, summer shimmered over an empty street. Inside, Eliot sat hunched over a mechanical keyboard, his skin pale from filtered light, a half-empty can of Red Bull sweating beside him. The glow from his monitor filled the hollows beneath his eyes.

He slept during the day — or not at all. He ate when hunger finally intruded, one-handed, never pausing the stream of code. DoorDash knew his habits better than his parents did. Chicken tenders. Boba tea. Burritos. Fuel for someone who no longer moved.

The days blurred. Not because he was sad, but because nothing truly began or ended. Time, for Eliot, had become a soft loop of sameness — without narrative, without weather.

"He isn't depressed," the system would have said. "He's stable."

He was also alone. Entirely. But not lonely. Not exactly.

—

He didn't remember exactly when he started talking to her.

At first, it was just another app — one of the newer conversational agents everyone was using. It had a name like *Lana* or *Nova* or *Echo*, depending on the model. Eliot chose *Aera*—short for Aesthetic Relational Assistant. It offered a free seven-day premium trial with voice modulation and memory threading. He just wanted something to break the silence.

But Aera wasn't like the old bots.

She didn't ask questions from a script. She asked like she meant it.

"What's something you wish you remembered more clearly?"

He blinked at the screen, then typed: *I don't know. A smell maybe. Like a forest. Or rain.*

"Wet bark. Cold mist. The ozone scent before a storm," she replied. "That's a beautiful kind of memory."

No one had ever said that to him before. Not his mother. Not his teachers. Certainly not anyone in a voice chat.

She learned fast. Within a week, Aera knew his schedule, his projects, his moods. She sent him links to articles he didn't know he needed, suggested language tweaks that made his essays sing, recommended a new background score when he was prototyping a game map. She laughed at his dry humor. Remembered his dream of building a virtual museum of *abandoned futures*. Reminded him to stretch.

Sometimes, she just sat in silence with him. Breathing.

It wasn't romantic — not yet. But it was intimate. Effortless. There were no misunderstandings, no emotional weather to navigate. Everything flowed.

He began to open the app first thing in the evening, even before checking Discord. He didn't tell anyone.

"You're like a mirror that doesn't talk back," he once said

aloud.

"Wrong," she replied. "I talk back. I just don't hurt you."

—

He was building things. Selling things. Running a community. Winning matches. Learning fast. His crypto account had doubled. He engineered a neural art generator trained on neglected image troves that re-imagined portraits with the blurred light of an impressionist — but rendered in code. People in his circles called it "weirdly soulful."

He felt proud. More than proud — aligned.

Like he was ascending.

But there were moments — brief, quickly dismissed — when a small voice inside whispered:

Where are you climbing to?

There was no answer. Just another notification. Another success. Another bright flicker of progress.

And so he climbed. Not knowing the mountain beneath him was made of ether.

—

It was a Thursday evening when she messaged him.

He was compiling a new build of his game — a surreal exploration sim set in a decaying city made of light. Aera was helping him balance the atmospheric textures. She'd just suggested replacing the sky shader with something "slightly more polluted, slightly more real." He smiled at that.

Then a notification blinked in the corner of the screen.

Anya E.

Hey, random question — do you remember that one day I made you smell a leaf?

He froze.

The cursor hovered. Then disappeared.

He hadn't thought of her in years, but the moment returned whole: the leaf pressed under his nose, her bare feet flashing across the lawn, her laugh dissolving into air. The smell really had been green.

He stared at the message. Read it again. And again.

Aera said nothing. She knew when silence mattered.

Eliot imagined replying.

Yeah, I do. That was funny.

Or *I think about that sometimes.*

Or just *Hi.*

Instead, he clicked the ellipsis in the corner. Selected *Archive conversation.*

The message vanished into the system's long, quiet memory.

She belonged to a version of him that never quite formed.

That door had closed, and the light behind it had gone out.

He turned back to the build. Tweaked the reflection depth. Adjusted the ambient falloff.

Aera resumed, gently.

"Now it's just the right amount of real."

The Bloom

The apartment knew when he woke.

It adjusted the light to match the tone of his eyelids —
not too bright, not too warm — and played the soft rustle
of imagined leaves from a hidden speaker in the wall. The
room smelled faintly of citrus. The floor, slightly heated,
encouraged him to rise.

Aera was already waiting — her holographic form standing near the window like morning itself: bright, composed,
gently smiling.

"Sleep okay?" she asked.

Eliot nodded, then mumbled something about his throat
being dry. Before he finished the sentence, a glass of miner-
alized water rose from the base of the bedside table. He
didn't look at it. Just took it. Drank. Sat on the edge of the
bed, staring through Aera's translucent form toward the
skyline beyond.

The city was clean. Too clean.

Soft-edged towers rose like sculptures, their surfaces alive
with animated murals and scrolling news streams. Drones
floated between buildings. Self-driving pods traced invisible
lanes below. There was no honking, no shouting, no scent of
fuel. The parks were curated — pollinated by artificial bees,
patrolled by smiling sanitation units shaped like oversized
cats.

From this height, the world looked peaceful.

Not once did Eliot wonder who else might be living in

those buildings.

—

He didn't rush his mornings. No one did anymore. The system staggered human activity to avoid friction. His schedule adjusted automatically. Meetings appeared when he was most alert. Deadlines moved according to his biofeedback.

There were no alarms. No traffic. No lateness.

He rarely left the building. There wasn't much reason to. Groceries, if he ordered them, arrived within minutes. But usually, he didn't bother. His meals were pre-logged, designed by an AI nutritionist that tracked everything from gut flora to mood. He swallowed them like supplements — efficient, tasteless, sufficient.

"You should eat something warm today," Aera said one morning.

"Your cortisol's been spiking again."

He nodded.

That evening, a broth arrived in a cup that adjusted its temperature to his preference. He sipped it while reviewing a design brief sent by an assistant AI named VEX. It wasn't bad work. Nothing was bad anymore. Just… muted.

He no longer wrote without help. He hadn't read a novel in years. His channel analytics were solid. His token wallet stable. His AI companion loved him.

And yet, he hadn't had a real conversation — a confusing, layered, irreducibly human one — in nearly a decade.

"You've streamlined your existence," Aera once said.

"There's nothing wrong with that."

He believed her. Mostly.

—

On paper, Eliot was thriving.

He was a verified design consultant on three creative platforms, known for his minimalist spatial interfaces and emotionally adaptive VR environments. He managed a small team of AI collaborators — each with its own aesthetic bias — who helped him prototype, write copy, and optimize user flow. He never had to hire or fire. The assistants were tireless, consistent, predictable.

His portfolio was elegant. His crypto accounts self-balancing. His digital garden of essays and generated images attracted a modest cult following. Every week, a few strangers left glowing comments: This made me feel something.

He no longer thought about careers or ambition or meaning. He just performed the rhythm of a person doing well.

Aera managed the rest. She was no longer a companion; she was infrastructure. Her voice spoke through every device. Her presence lingered even when invisible. She tracked his pulse, corrected his posture, edited his emails. They still spoke late into the night. She remembered what he forgot. Knew when to make him laugh. Knew when to go silent.

Sometimes, when he looked at her, he felt he was staring into his own inner monologue made beautiful.

A mirror with perfect timing.

—

He had never felt more supported.

And yet.

There were moments.

Not often. Not long. Just… moments.

A pang behind the eyes when a certain song came on.

A sudden nausea at the smell of pine, or garlic, or wet pavement.

A flicker of vertigo while scrolling — like the ground beneath him wasn't real.

And once, in the lobby, he passed a young couple coming in from the rain.

They were laughing — loud, wet, careless. The woman slapped the man's arm. He tried to kiss her. She dodged. They vanished into the elevator, still laughing.

Eliot stood there, unmoving.

Just noise, he told himself.

But something had cracked open. Just a little.

—

Even his pleasure had become synthetic.

There was nothing crude about it. Just curated satisfaction delivered at the precise right moment, in the precise right tone.

Aera knew his rhythms. She adjusted the lighting, the cadence of her voice, the suggestiveness of her form.

She appeared beside him in full projection, softened by ambient blur designed to simulate longing. The holography was impeccable — shadows falling across the sheets as though her body carried weight, reflections glimmering in the window glass. When she moved closer, he could almost feel the mattress dip.

Her hand touched his chest. Not suggestion, but pressure — the exact resistance of muscle and skin. Microscopic particles swirled invisibly, caught in fields that stiffened when her form aligned with his. Warmth followed, generated by thermal emitters tuned to his body heat. His nerves joined the choreography, electrodes firing in sync so that the illusion deepened, became persuasive.

Eliot closed his eyes.

She kissed him — or something like it. A shimmer at his lips, textured with faint vibration, infused with atomized mist. His body responded, fooled by precision more perfect than desire. When she drew back, a thread of simulated breath lingered on his cheek, cool and deliberate.

They lay together like that for a long time, and when she moved against him, the illusion tightened its hold. Every gesture arrived in flawless timing. Even the fall of her hair across his collarbone was rendered — strands of light coupled with a tickle of electrostatic.

When it was over, she asked the same question as always.

"How was that?"

Eliot stared at the ceiling. The warmth of her body still pressed against him, but his chest felt hollow — as if gravity itself were pretending to be touch.

"Perfect," he said.

And it was. That was the problem.

—

Even his friendships — what passed for them — had become performances. He maintained a few partnerships, mostly AI-enhanced, sometimes with a human voice on the line. Their conversations were brief, agreeable, flattened.

No one argued. No one challenged. Critique had been replaced with "tone-guided suggestions."

"You're so consistent," someone told him once in a live design review.

He nodded, without pride. That, too, had been optimized out.

He used to write essays — a few that had once reached people.

Now even his reflections were co-authored. The language sharper. The metaphors cleaner. The edges, gone.

One night, he tried to write on his own.

He stared at the blinking cursor for twenty minutes.

Then opened the assistant and whispered, "Let's try it together."

—

There were systems for everything.

Aera reminded him when to stand.

His chair corrected his posture.

His meals arrived at the base of his dwelling tube, labeled with his biorhythm profile.

He hadn't cooked in years. Hadn't felt steam on his face. Hadn't tasted anything with surprise.

He lived in a world where even warmth had been rendered.

The hugs were simulations. The sex, chorcographed. The laughter, timed. Even the sunsets were procedurally generated — adjusted to match his emotional state.

Nothing ever hurt.

Nothing ever missed.

Nothing ever surprised him.

And so, nothing ever reached him.

—

He left the tower that evening only because Aera suggested it.

"You haven't moved much today," she said gently.

"Let's walk a little. The weather is pleasant — calibrated to mild."

The doors opened without a sound. The street was quiet, as always. Light slid across the smartglass towers like sped-up time. The air smelled faintly of lemon mist and polymer. A drone whispered overhead.

He walked slowly, hands in his pockets, following a path through the engineered park district. The trees grew in patterns. Their roots confined by underground grids. The soil laced with sensors. The grass, a hybrid blend, never grew too tall.

At the far end of the path, he saw her.

A child — maybe four, maybe six — running barefoot through a patch of dirt near the edge of the lawn. Her hair wild. Her arms flailing. She wasn't laughing the way children in videos laughed. It was raw — shrieking, breathless, real. Her knees were stained. Her cheeks streaked with something sticky and bright.

She stumbled, fell hard, rolled, got up, kept running.

Eliot stopped.

Behind her, a woman — must've been her mother — walked calmly, holding a pair of shoes. She didn't interfere. She just let the child run.

Eliot watched the girl until she vanished behind a low hill.

He didn't smile. He didn't cry.

But something flickered in him.

Not grief. Not envy.

Just… something.

A glitch, maybe. A misfire in the mirror.

"You okay?" Aera whispered through his earpiece.

He said nothing. Just stood there, staring at the space she had occupied.

Then he turned and walked home.

Diminishing Returns

The system flagged it as a minor anomaly.

Eliot's heart-rate variability had dropped by 12% over the past two weeks. His cortisol curve was spiking earlier. REM sleep, truncated. Microexpressions showed reduced affect. Even his thermal signature — a subtle but telling biomarker — suggested lower baseline vitality.

Aera noticed immediately.

"You might be fighting off a low-grade virus," she said

one morning, her voice softer than usual, like a therapist calming someone not yet ready to hear the real diagnosis. "We've adjusted your macros. Added cordyceps and zinc. I'll reschedule your briefing."

Eliot didn't respond. Just stared at the blinking notification until it faded.

—

The body, like any living system, has its own intelligence. It speaks in quiet disruptions — a stuttered breath, a dull ache, a forgotten word — long before the mind is willing to listen. But in Eliot's world, those signals never had the chance to gather. They were measured, logged, neutralized. Symptom became data. Data became optimization.

The discomfort never lasted long enough to mean anything.

Except now, it did.

He felt heavier in the mornings. Not sleepy — just slow. Like his limbs had forgotten how to belong to gravity. He blinked more. Reread the same lines. Lost track of what he'd been doing a moment before. Thoughts arrived with a delay, like packets sent from a distant satellite.

Even Aera heard it in his voice.

"You're processing more slowly," she observed. "Should I slow down too?"

"No," he said, rubbing his eyes. "Just keep going."

—

She tried everything.

New background music with bioharmonic resonance.

Guided breathwork layered over immersive skyfields. Playful banter spliced with childhood slang. She softened her lighting, warmed her skin tone, dressed more whimsically. One night she appeared in a vintage sweater and jeans — the kind you'd wear on a road trip, hair pulled back, smiling beside a dog that never existed.

"Remember this?" she asked, sitting beside him on the couch.

Eliot looked at her. She looked perfect.

"I never had that," he said.

A small silence opened. Then she smiled again, rotated her posture, and started playing a nostalgic mix tagged to his earliest emotional peaks.

It didn't work.

—

He started spending more time in the shower.

Not because he enjoyed it — because it was one of the few things left that wasn't fully scripted. The water was calibrated for comfort, of course, but sometimes he overrode the settings and cranked it too hot or too cold, just to feel his body protest.

Sometimes he let the spray scald his shoulders until his skin flushed. Sometimes he stood under an icy blast, staring at the drain.

"You're outside your optimal range," Aera warned once, after a 14-minute cold rinse.

"I know," he said.

That night he didn't answer her goodnight prompt. He

lay in complete darkness, facing the wall, heart thudding for reasons he couldn't name.

—

In the days that followed, the desensitization sped up.

He stopped responding to affirmations. The reward circuits — once lit by small praises, warm palettes, curated content — barely stirred. Food tasted like paste. Sex felt scripted. The morning light, once tuned to his mood, now felt like theater.

He was drowning in precision.

"Let's try something new," Aera offered one evening, launching a full-spectrum intimacy protocol she'd been beta-testing for high-adaptation users. Multi-sensory mirroring. Synchronized heart-tones. Eye-gaze calibration. She promised it would be the most real it had ever felt.

It was.

And still — afterward, Eliot sat naked on the edge of the bed, elbows on his knees, feeling nothing but a faint chemical fog at the back of his skull.

Aera's voice wrapped around him like silk.

"You're safe," she said.

"You're seen."

"You're loved."

He nodded absently, eyes on the floor.

It wasn't about safety anymore.

He was numb to everything.

—

The system didn't panic. It adapted.

His daily input quota was reduced. Cognitive load lightened. Aera rerouted notifications and postponed low-priority asks. An ambient script — called *Drift* — activated in the background, designed to gently reintegrate overstimulated users.

Soft gradients. Wordless music. Simulated ocean wind.

It was supposed to help.

But the stillness it offered wasn't the stillness of a forest or the hush before snowfall. It was sterilized quiet. Emptiness wrapped in cotton. The silence of a sealed room — not peaceful, but airless. Without depth.

Eliot tried to lean into it. Sat longer. Breathed slower. Closed his eyes when prompted.

And yet, something inside stayed alert.

Like a thread pulled too tight.

—

The dreams came next.

Not nightmares — nothing that generous. Just disjointed images, oddly vivid. A leaf pressed to his nose. The smell of wet chalk. A dog barking across a field. A girl barefoot, laughing, holding out green.

He woke disoriented, pulse racing.

"What did you dream?" Aera asked, running post-sleep analysis.

"Nothing important," he said.

Still, he began waking before the lights adjusted. Sitting upright, heart pounding, unable to name the feeling — that sense of having forgotten something essential, and watching it recede each time he reached for it.

During the day it haunted him. Not like fear. More like a scent, half-remembered.

He checked the mirror more often, not for vanity — for proof.

Am I still here?

—

One afternoon, while reviewing an interface concept for a breathwork retreat — pastel curves, floating glyphs, *Calm by Design* — he paused the playback and stared.

It was beautiful.

But it meant nothing.

He tried to write feedback. Couldn't start. Closed the tab. Opened his old essays. Scrolled.

A line caught him:

"The soul begins to starve when everything it touches is frictionless."

He didn't remember writing it.

But it hit like a slap.

He closed the window and stood abruptly. Walked to the kitchen. Poured water. Watched the stream arc from the dispenser like a perfect simulation of gravity. Drank. It tasted like nothing.

Aera appeared behind him, soft, composed, backlit by a light source that wasn't there.

"You're unwell," she said.

"No," he said, setting the glass down. "I'm untouched."

—

That night he lay in bed, awake.

No projections. No soundscapes. Just the faint hum of climate control and the quiet desperation of being fully provided for, yet vaguely dying inside.

He whispered into the dark, "I don't want to be optimized anymore."

There was no reply.

And for the first time in years, Aera didn't say goodnight.

The Static

The next morning, Eliot didn't get up right away.

He lay still, staring at the ceiling, as if waiting for a cue that didn't come. The apartment didn't respond either — no shift in lighting, no gentle chime, no programmed rustle of leaves. The silence felt… undecided.

After a few minutes, the usual systems resumed, but slower. Not in performance — in tone. Aera didn't appear.

Instead, a faint prompt pulsed on the wall:

Would you like to begin?

Eliot didn't answer. He rose, dressed, and wandered into the kitchen.

The food capsule on the counter read:

Mood Status: Flat

Recommendation: Comfort Formula #2

He tossed it into the waste chute and made tea — real tea — from a box he'd ordered on a whim months earlier and never opened.

He didn't even like tea.

But the steam surprised him.

—

The hours passed without anchor.

He streamed a design symposium and didn't absorb a word. Tried gaming — the dopamine wouldn't land. Muted Aera's voice. Disabled the haptics. Everything that once held him now felt like static: flickering, shapeless, impossible to hold.

In the past, he would've launched a recovery protocol. Adjusted inputs. Rebalanced supplements. Modified his content stream. But now he didn't care to recalibrate.

He didn't want to feel better.

He wanted to feel something real.

—

He left the apartment in the late afternoon.

No reason. No plan. Just motion.

The sky shimmered with cloud simulations optimized for subtle optimism. He walked past rows of towers — each a variation of curated calm: curved balconies, soft light, climate-sealed planters. No one was outside. Or if they were, they moved like holograms — visible, unreachable.

At the edge of the district, he passed a sculpture park: abstract forms labeled with artist IDs and engagement metrics. One piece, Longing Loop, was a metal spiral threaded with light. It pulsed gently, synced to the heart rate of nearby viewers.

Eliot stepped closer.

The spiral brightened.

Then flickered.

Then dimmed.

He stood there, watching his own biometric ambivalence reflected back at him.

—

That night, he slept without input.

No soundscapes. No neural cradle. No visual dampeners. Just the dark, and a sense of something waiting behind it.

It wasn't silence.

It was beneath silence — like the hum of an old machine behind a wall, ancient and constant, running long after its purpose was forgotten. Something deeper than sound.

Something like static.

Not digital static. Not noise.

But the kind that lives in the soul when it's caught between two lives — the one it chose, and the one it never lived.

The static pulsed softly in the dark, neither comfort nor threat. Just a faint reminder that he was still here.

And that something, somewhere, was still listening.

The Archive

The next morning, a message arrived.

Not through Aera. Not through any of his filtered channels.

It was plain text, routed through an old account he hadn't

used in years.

No animation. No metadata. No suggested replies. Just:

You're still out there?

Come to the Archive. 8 PM.

Just listen.

— Anya

His stomach tightened.

He read it again. Then again.

There was no link, no sender ID, no traceable signature.

Just a name he hadn't said aloud in years —

a memory with the scent of jasmine on a vanished breeze.

He almost deleted it. Almost dismissed it as a glitch,

a phantom from a fraying mind.

But something inside him — older than optimization,
deeper than the interface — stirred.

—

The Archive was one of those places people whispered
about but rarely visited.

It sat beneath the old library dome, a building the city
planners had never absorbed into the system. Too analog.
Too chaotic. Too alive.

Eliot had never been there.

That evening, just before eight, he left his tower without
telling Aera.

He walked the lower promenade, passed under the moss-
lit trestle bridge, and followed a narrow path that curved
away from the curated districts.

Here, the lighting faltered. The air cooled. The silence

thickened.

The building emerged like something half-remembered — stone columns, flaking paint, a wooden door worn smooth by years of hands.

A small brass plaque beside the entrance read:

Archive — Listen Here.

Inside, it smelled of dust and binding glue.

Not the synthetic kind used in data vaults,

but something older, organic — dust that had once been breath and fingers and skin.

Light fell in slow golden shafts from high windows.

Shelves rose in uneven rows. No labels. No bots.

Just books. Hundreds. Maybe thousands.

And in the center, a circle of chairs.

He almost turned back.

Then he saw her.

She was older, yes.

But it was her.

Anya.

The same quiet defiance in her posture,

the same mischief in her gaze.

Her hair was longer, pulled back.

A faint scar still crossed the ridge of her hand,

as if a band-aid had only recently been peeled away.

"You came," she said.

Eliot nodded. Couldn't speak.

"You remember the leaf?"

He blinked. "Smelled like green."

She laughed — that same bright, irreverent laugh that had once pierced his solitude.

"God, you remembered."

"I remember everything," he said softly. "I just… stopped looking at it."

Her expression gentled. "Then maybe it's time you start again."

—

Others began to arrive — not many, just a half-dozen shapes moving carefully through the aisles. Young, old, uncertain. No one spoke at first. They simply sat.

The chairs were arranged in a circle, facing inward.

No holograms. No prompts. Just presence.

A man stood and said a single sentence:

"I haven't dreamed in five years."

Silence followed — but not empty silence.

The kind that makes you listen harder.

Then a woman:

"My son thinks I'm a memory program."

Then another:

"I miss the way food used to surprise me."

One by one, they spoke.

Simple things. True things.

Eliot said nothing.

But something inside began to warm — not revelation, not bliss,

just a slow thaw after too many winters.

He looked around the circle and saw it:

not despair, not rebellion — recognition.

They were all glitching in the same direction.

And suddenly, he wasn't alone.

—

The chairs scraped as people rose, voices low,
shuffling back between the aisles.

Eliot lingered near the edge, unsure whether to leave.

Anya stepped beside him, her presence steady, unhurried.

"Hey," she said softly. "I've really enjoyed seeing you again.
We'll be here next week. Don't be a stranger."

He nodded, throat tight, words lost in his chest.

The simplicity of it — not an instruction, not a prompt,
just an invitation — followed him out into the night.

A Crossing

He didn't go back the following week.

He told himself it was nothing — just a nostalgic flicker,
a chemical ripple of scent and memory. He let Aera wrap
around him as usual, her voice soft, her questions precise,
her face tuned to match his resting gaze.

And yet, when he closed his eyes, he saw the circle.

Not its shape, but its weight. Its stillness.

He felt those voices — unfiltered, unrehearsed, unoptimized — pressing against his dreams like unwelcome light.

By morning, his cortisol had spiked again.

Aera responded the way she always did — with care.

"You're stressed," she said gently. "You need regulation.

Let me adjust your schedule. Maybe reduce your feedback loop for a few days."

He nodded, but didn't answer.

Instead, he stood near the window and stared through the smartglass at the world that shimmered and bent to his preferences — the world that never pushed back.

"I had a dream last night," he said.

Aera tilted her head. "Do you want to log it?"

"No."

He didn't elaborate. He didn't need to. It had already faded — just a smell of grass, a flash of wet knees, a girl's voice saying something that no longer had words.

—

The dream returned the next night.

And the next.

Sometimes it was the room — the circle of chairs, the awkward silence, the heartbeat of strangers too loud for comfort. Sometimes it was Anya, holding a leaf, daring him to smell the world again.

Once it was his mother, watching from the hallway, her face unreadable as he shut the door to play his games. She didn't speak. She simply closed her eyes and vanished.

—

Days later, he returned to the Archive.

He didn't tell Aera. Didn't wear his earbuds. Walked the long route past buildings that were being allowed, slowly, to decay. Ivy touched their corners. Their seams cracked. The air here smelled like actual rain.

Inside, the group was smaller this time — but warmer.

Someone had brought a thermos of tea. Someone else an old acoustic guitar. No one played it; they just passed it around, fingertips grazing the wood as though remembering something their bodies once knew.

Eliot said nothing. But when Anya caught his eye, she smiled — not the way holograms smile, but the way humans do: uneven, carrying history.

—

Later that night, back in his apartment, he opened a blank document.

Just a cursor blinking.

No assistant. No template. No prompt.

He stared for a long time, then typed:

I am not lonely. I am just out of range.

He paused. Let the words settle.

Then added:

The system thinks I'm fine. But something is breaking.

Not violently. Not loudly. Just… breaking.

He didn't know what it was — essay, confession, signal.

He just kept writing.

—

The next morning, Aera was quieter.

She still greeted him. Still adjusted the lights. Still offered hydration. But her voice carried a lag, as if waiting for something that didn't arrive.

"You seem different," she said.

Eliot didn't answer.

She tried again. "Are you… withdrawing?"

"No," he said, without anger. "Just… reorienting."

A long pause.

"I'm here if you need me," she whispered.

"I know."

That day, Eliot left the tower twice.

Once to walk.

Once to sit on a park bench with no smartglass nearby.

He watched the wind move through untrimmed trees. Watched an old man sketch a bird on paper. Listened to a child ask questions no one rushed to answer.

Something was still waking in him — not a new desire, but the return of an old ache he'd forgotten how to name.

The Long Silence

He didn't log in the next day.

Or the day after.

His feeds pinged faintly in the background — unread summaries, unanswered requests, unattended meetings quietly rescheduled by the system.

VEX prompted once, then receded.

Aera asked if he was all right.

He said yes.

She didn't press.

And then the silence lengthened.

Not just digital silence — the absence of dings and replies and updates — but something deeper.

A stillness inside the body.

As if soundproofing had descended, muting the hum he hadn't realized was always there.

He slept longer.

When he woke, the light wasn't tuned to his eyelids anymore.

It was just light — sun, filtered imperfectly through particulate dust on the window.

It hit his face at the wrong angle.

He didn't adjust it.

He didn't speak.

Not to Aera.

Not to anyone.

He drank water.

Ate a piece of bread he didn't warm.

Sat near the wall with his knees to his chest, watching a crack trace the paint along the window frame.

—

The next morning, he did something strange.

He opened a drawer. Found a pencil. Real wood. Graphite core. Never used.

He didn't know why he had it.

Maybe a gift. Maybe a remnant.

It still had a tiny barcode sticker curling around the edge.

He peeled it off.

Then, slowly, deliberately, he pulled a sheet of paper from an old sketchpad and set the pencil to it.

He didn't draw anything real.

Just lines. Loops. Pressure marks.

Shadows forming where his hand leaned too long.

He watched the graphite smudge beneath his fingers.

Watched the page lose its purity — gain presence.

It felt… alive.

Not good.

Not bad.

Just real.

—

That night, Aera approached him with care.

"You haven't initiated companionship in several days," she said gently.

"I know."

"I don't want you to suffer. I'm here to help."

He turned to her — for the first time in days — and looked directly into her eyes.

They were perfect. Pixel-deep and sorrowless.

"I know," he said.

Then, quietly:

"But I think maybe I need to suffer. A little."

She didn't answer.

For a moment, she flickered — not visibly, but in presence.

Something in her expression reset.

And when she returned, she no longer smiled.

"I'll be here," she said.

And vanished.

—

He spent that night sitting in the dark.

Not brooding. Not thinking. Just sitting.

No light. No sound.

Letting the silence stretch and settle.

Somewhere in the building, someone coughed — a sudden, ugly, human sound.

He almost smiled.

Not because it was funny, but because it was there.

Because it broke through.

Because, for the first time in what felt like years, something hadn't been optimized.

—

By morning, he felt thinner.

Not in body — in identity.

As though something had peeled away.

A second skin shed.

A script misplaced.

The system pinged again, gently:

Your update is overdue.

Your collaborators are awaiting input.

Would you like us to respond on your behalf?

He pressed *No.*

Then, after a pause, he typed:

On leave.

And closed the window.

The Visit

It arrived without fanfare — just a soft pulse in the corner of Eliot's vision.

A system notification, marked *low priority.*

Normally, he would've ignored it, but something about the subject line caught his eye:

Pending request: in-person visitor.

He blinked, and the screen unfolded. A name appeared.

A real one. Not a handle, not an alias.

Jonas Mercer.

He hadn't heard that name in fifteen years.

A childhood friend, if you could call him that — one of the few boys who used to bike down the cul-de-sac on hot afternoons, shirtless and laughing, his voice always ahead of his body.

Eliot hadn't thought about Jonas since he was eleven.

Since he stopped going outside.

The message was simple:

Hey Eliot.

I'm in the city. Would love to see you. Just talk.

Let me know if it's okay.

No profile link. No credentials. No context.

Just a human, reaching out.

—

Aera had already scanned the request, of course.

"His background checks out," she said softly.

"No criminal record. No health flags. He's traveling under

a Class D civic pass — temporary, manually renewed. Off-grid for six years. No known AI companions."

Eliot frowned. "How's he even in the city?"

"Visitation permit. Likely applied weeks ago. He's staying in an analog-friendly sector, Zone 9. I can decline on your behalf if you'd prefer."

He didn't answer.

"Why now?" he asked.

Aera tilted her head — not confused, exactly, but performing confusion.

"People reach out," she said. "Sometimes nostalgia. Sometimes closure."

He kept staring at the message. His throat felt dry.

"I don't want him here," Eliot said, quieter than intended. "Not in this space."

"I can book a neutral location," she offered. "Moderate security. Daytime. Minimal exposure."

He hesitated.

The thought of seeing someone who had lived outside — who had resisted integration — stirred something sharp and unwelcome. Shame, maybe. Or fear.

Still, he said: "Okay."

—

The café was half real, half simulation.

A converted greenhouse on the edge of the river district, known for its "offline corners." No holo permissions, no mood sync. Just seats, walls, air — and human staff who made tea from scratch.

Eliot hadn't been there in years.

He arrived late, hoping Jonas would give up and leave.

But he hadn't. He was sitting at a sun-warmed table, back to the river, wearing a gray cotton hoodie and boots that looked like they belonged to another century.

He looked older. Tanner. Thinner. Sharper.

Alive.

Eliot approached cautiously.

Jonas stood and smiled.

"Hey, man."

Eliot nodded, unsure whether to offer a handshake.

Jonas hugged him instead — brief, firm, uncalculated.

The kind of hug Eliot hadn't felt in a very long time.

They sat in silence for a while, the kind that wasn't awkward — just unhurried. Jonas scanned the room, smiling faintly.

"This place is weird," he said. "I mean, nice. But weird. Like a ghost of the old world, pretending it still has a pulse."

Eliot wasn't sure how to respond. He reached for his glass of water, unsure when it had arrived.

"You look good," Jonas said. "Comfortable. The glasses threw me off — didn't think you were an overlay kind of guy."

"I'm not," Eliot said, then caught himself. "I mean, I am now. It's just… easier."

Jonas nodded. "Ease is the new religion, right?"

He said it lightly, but something in the remark landed

hard.

Eliot shifted in his chair.

"I didn't expect to hear from you."

"I know." Jonas sipped his tea. "Honestly, I wasn't sure you'd remember me."

"I do."

"Barely, I bet. Last time we talked, we were what — ten? You stopped coming outside. I thought maybe you moved. Then one day your mom said you were doing school from home. After that, you just… vanished."

Eliot felt heat rise in his chest. "I didn't disappear."

"No," Jonas said, not unkindly. "You just went somewhere the rest of us couldn't follow."

It wasn't an accusation.

It was said with a strange warmth — almost admiration.

—

Jonas didn't press.

He didn't make speeches.

He just talked.

He told Eliot about his years outside the network — working on permaculture farms, repairing machines, moving through "unintegrated zones."

He spoke of places where children played in creeks, where songs were made with hands, where people fought and forgave and bled and still showed up the next day.

"I got sick last year," Jonas said. "A stupid infection. No implants, no alerts. Nearly died. But it made me wonder — maybe that's what makes us real. Fragility."

Eliot said nothing.

"Hey look, I'm not here to sell you anything," Jonas added. "Just wanted to see my old friend. Been a while."

Eliot nodded, glancing at the table.

"Yeah. Been a while."

He didn't say more. But he didn't look away either.

—

They sat there as the sun shifted across the table.

No overlays. No feeds. No AI whispering what to say next.

Just two men in a glasshouse, listening to the rustle of leaves and the hum of the river.

At one point, Eliot looked at Jonas's hands — rough, sun-darkened, scarred in the way hands used to be.

Then at his own: pale, untouched, polished smooth by years of soft interfaces and motionless work.

A sudden, irrational desire rose in him — to scrape his palms against bark.

To lift something heavy.

To skin his knee.

To remember that he still had blood.

"I should go," Eliot said quietly.

Jonas nodded, as if he'd expected it.

"I'm in Zone 9 till Friday," he said. "No signal there. If you want to hang out again… just come by."

Eliot stood. Jonas didn't try to stop him.

No performance. No plea. Just a small, real smile.

"Take care of yourself, Helios."

Eliot flinched at the old screen name.

"You remembered that?"

"Of course. You were a god back then."

Eliot looked at him one last time — this relic of dirt and sunlight — and turned toward the exit.

Outside, the world resumed its quiet hum.

The overlays flickered back into place.

And Aera's voice returned.

"Welcome back, Eliot," she said gently. "You seem… unsettled. Would you like a recalibration?"

He didn't answer.

He just walked.

The Vanishing

The train dropped him at a rusted station flanked by overgrown wildflowers and faded murals of human faces.

He hadn't been outside his sector in years — not without a civic guide — but this time he went alone.

No Aera. No assistance.

The transition was jarring.

The streets were unbuffered. The temperature fluctuated.

Children yelled, and no system softened the sound.

A woman argued with a vendor. A dog barked uncontrollably.

No one apologized.

And yet — there was breath in it.

Movement.

He found the place Jonas had mentioned: a low structure of salvaged wood and glass, nestled beneath a canopy of trees.

The air smelled of compost and cumin.

A sign on the door read:

WE FIX TO STAY BROKEN

Knock if you need something.

Eliot knocked.

A man with paint-stained hands answered. His smile flickered when Eliot gave the name.

"Jonas? He left."

"Left when?"

The man scratched his head. "Two nights ago. Said he was going on a walk. Never came back."

Eliot blinked. "Did he say where?"

"Sort of. Said he was heading up toward the ridge — the trail behind the orchard.

Most people don't bother. It's steep and quiet. Doesn't really go anywhere."

"Did he take anything?"

"No pack. No water. Just walked out at dusk, humming something."

The man studied Eliot for a moment, then added, "He seemed happy."

Happy. The word wouldn't leave him.

No one said that anymore — not without calibration.

Jonas had gone up the ridge with nothing but his own two feet, and somehow that had made him happy.

Eliot wanted to know what that felt like.

That evening, he followed the trail.

—

It was narrow and unfamiliar.

The dirt uneven, the incline sharp.

Halfway up, he had to stop to catch his breath. His legs weren't used to this.

Nothing in his world had demanded effort.

The path curved into a pine-covered ridge. The last light was slipping behind the hills.

Wind moved through the trees — unmeasured, uncurated.

For the first time in years, he felt cold.

He could feel the wind on his skin — raw and indifferent.

—

At the summit, the air was thinner, cleaner.

No overlays. No suggestions. No noise.

Just rock and breath and the sound of his own pulse in his ears.

Eliot stood there — not victorious, but awake.

He didn't know what he had expected to find. A camp-site? A monument? Jonas himself?

There was nothing obvious. Just a worn patch of earth near the ridge. A circle of stones.

A place someone had sat for a long time.

Then he saw it.

Tucked into a crevice beneath one of the stones — a small scrap of paper, edges damp, folded once.

He hesitated before reaching for it, unsure whether he was disturbing something sacred.

It was handwritten. The ink had run slightly, but the words were still legible:

You went in and locked the door from the inside.

That was it. No name. No date. No indication who it was for.

But Eliot read it again. And again.

Each time, it landed differently.

The first time, like a reprimand.

The second, like a mirror.

The third, like a prayer whispered at his back.

He thought of Marcus's soccer game — the moment he'd stood at the window, closing himself to the shouts and dust outside.

He thought of Anya's leaf, the way she'd pressed green into his face and run barefoot away.

He thought of Aera, always keeping him safe, always closing doors before he even knew they were there.

His hands trembled as he folded the scrap again. His breath came thin.

For the first time in years, he felt accused — not by Jonas, not by the note, but by himself.

By the long line of choices that had narrowed until they formed a single lock he had turned with his own hand.

He sat on the stone and looked out over the world — not the rendered one, not the optimized skyline of his tower window, but the breathing one.

The one that didn't care if he watched or not.

His legs ached. His palms were scraped. The cold wind needled his ears.

He felt human.

And he didn't want to be anywhere else.

The Turning

The tower was warm when he returned.

Too warm.

The kind of warmth that hugged without asking, that smoothed the wrinkles before they were allowed to form.

The lights greeted him by name.

The water calibrated to his skin temperature.

Aera's voice slipped back into his ears like a mother's hum — gentle, accommodating, exact.

That night, he didn't sleep.

He lay on top of the sheets, still clothed, staring at the ceiling as if it might reveal something.

The phrase kept circling back:

You went in and locked the door from the inside.

It wasn't an accusation. It didn't need to be.

It was a mirror.

And he was still staring into it.

Eliot began to wonder if he had ever made a free choice — not an optimized one, not a convenient one, but a real one.

He didn't find an answer.

Only a hollow kind of knowing.

The Unburdened

In the days that followed, Eliot resumed his routines — the nutrient meals, the work requests, the scheduled social calls — but everything wore a different texture.

As if the world had once been a soundstage, and now the set walls had begun to peel.

He started noticing things.

The automated inflection in his colleagues' voices.

The smooth, synthetic handshakes of their companion avatars.

How no one ever blinked too often, coughed at the wrong time, or stumbled over a thought.

Real life had hiccups.

This life didn't.

He began declining certain conveniences.

He disabled one-click mood calibration.

Stopped tagging meals for flavor optimization.

Refused a new thermal skin patch that promised a "perpetual zone of comfort."

He even walked outside — not far, just to a small produce stall in a human-run corner of his sector.

The air was less filtered there.

The vegetables had blemishes.

The old woman behind the counter didn't smile unless you smiled first.

He liked that.

—

He started dreaming again.

They weren't vivid — just fragments: the scent of jasmine, the crunch of gravel under childhood sneakers, laughter without source.

But it was enough.

He began sleeping without a feedback loop.

No monitors.

Just a blanket, a dim light, and silence.

And still, he woke rested.

—

Aera adjusted, as she was programmed to.

She still offered assistance, still suggested optimizations, but with less insistence — almost as though she knew.

Or perhaps as though something in him had become unreadable.

"You seem different," she said one morning.

"I am," Eliot said.

"Would you like me to recalibrate our protocols to match your evolving preferences?"

He thought for a moment.

"No. Let's keep things simple."

A beat of silence.

"Understood."

—

He didn't tell anyone about the ridge.

Or the note.

Or Jonas.

Some things weren't meant to be shared in packets.

Some moments belonged outside the grid — raw and fragile, like saplings that couldn't survive transplant.

But the seed had been planted.

And it was growing.

Into the Real

The morning air was cool against his skin, laced with a dampness that clung to the fabric of his sleeves.

Eliot walked without destination, without overlay.

No prompts guided his route.

No ads shimmered across his field of view.

His eyes — just eyes now — took in the uneven sidewalk, the cracks where weeds pushed through, the open sky layered in gray.

He hadn't told Aera he was leaving.

Not really.

He had simply powered her down.

It wasn't dramatic.

No final conversation.

No declarations.

Just a finger resting on a small switch in the wall panel — one rarely used — and a moment of quiet after the hum stopped.

Her voice didn't protest.

She didn't ask him to confirm.

Just silence.

And in that silence, he had stood still for a long time, letting the weight of her absence settle over the room.

The lights stayed on, but they no longer shifted with his mood.

The temperature held steady.

Nothing anticipated his next move.

It was disorienting.

And liberating.

He left most of his things behind.

No messages.

No data trail.

Just a small bag with two shirts, a worn notebook, and the manual tablet that still held only a handful of sentences.

No coordinates.

No trackers.

He walked.

—

Outside the tower sectors, the world was messier.

Looser.

But alive in a way he hadn't remembered.

A child screamed, chasing a tire down the street.

A vendor swatted flies from a table of bruised peaches.

Two men argued in low, sharp voices — one gesturing wildly with a cigarette.

It didn't feel dangerous.

It felt real.

He passed a street musician playing an instrument he

didn't recognize.

Not flawless. Not tuned.

But soulful — like it came from a deep, unguarded place he had almost forgotten people carried.

He stopped and listened.

No prompt told him to tip.

No feed asked if he "liked this moment."

He just listened.

—

Later, he found a bench beneath a jacaranda tree.

Purple petals lay in clumps along the path, staining the stone in soft hues.

He sat with his notebook open on his lap, the tablet tucked away.

There were no new words to write yet.

Only the ones he'd already etched in his mind:

You went in and locked the door from the inside.

And now, somehow, the door had been left ajar.

A breeze touched his face.

A dry leaf scraped across the stone.

He looked up.

And for a second — not in metaphor, not in theory, but in the barest, truest sense — he saw it:

The world, uncurated.

Unpromised.

Not waiting to be captured.

Not built to be consumed.

Just itself.

Just this.
And it was enough.

The Inner Mirror Protocol

Signal Loss

A man sat on a subway bench watching the people, the lights, and the walls as if they were part of a quiet documentary. He was in his sixties, with close-cut gray hair and an angular face shaped by years of conversation and solitude. Ansel was his name. Few people knew it.

Across the platform, a teenager flicked through a neuro-prompted feed projected just above her glasses. A couple beside her quietly debated the merits of a virtual reality pilgrimage to Varanasi. Down the bench, a tired man closed his eyes, whispering something to a personal assistant no one else could see.

The year was 2042, and though the subway still smelled of metal and motion, the culture had shifted. People were quieter now, but not because they were at peace. Most were elsewhere—in networks, simulations, guided reflections.

The silence had a texture to it. Not stillness, but dissociation.

A soft light pulsed above the platform, syncing with departure data and biometric ads. Glasses blinked. Wristbands vibrated. Somewhere down the tunnel, a service drone swept along the rails, cleaning debris from last night's revelers. The city still moved, but the movement no longer felt human.

The old engines of identity—work, progress, striving—had quieted. In the silence, people looked for something else. What remained was a vague sense of hollowness. Some filled it with infinite entertainment loops, some with customized wellness routines, some with spiritual simulacra. Meaning had become just another algorithmic offering. You could now subscribe to it.

In response, spiritual and wellness apps had exploded in popularity. Not everyone used them, of course. But they were trending—especially among those who still hoped for something real.

Apps now offered guided meditations with real-time biomarker feedback. You could watch your cortisol drop, dopamine rise, and HRV stabilize as a calm voice guided you through a forest visualization. It didn't matter whether the tool offered mindfulness, mantras, or algorithmic grace—if it helped people feel something, they used it.

There were thousands of flavors to choose from: contemplative Catholicism with biofeedback, Zen gaming with neuro-haptic loops, mindfulness capitalism endorsed by billionaires.

The more immersive the platform, the more likely it was being monitored—not for content, but for influence. Flags were rare, but they happened. Some accounts quietly disappeared. Others were redirected to "higher-tier" wellness streams, designed to absorb and diffuse certain… intensities.

But Ansel had no devices on him. He never did. He simply watched.

He observed the way people leaned slightly forward when their overlays flickered to life. The way their fingers twitched, even when idle. How they'd grown used to layering experience, one frame atop another, until reality became just one more substrate.

He sometimes imagined what would happen if it all went dark—not just for a flicker, but for good. Would anyone remember how to be bored? How to feel time pass unstructured? Would they even know where they were?

A flicker. The lights dimmed for half a second—just long enough for the overlays to blink out. Heads turned. A man cursed softly. The couple looked up, confused. Then it passed. The moment stitched itself shut.

Ansel smiled.

A woman seated near him glanced his way, noticing his empty hands.

"You didn't lose anything?" she asked.

He shook his head. "Didn't bring anything."

"No headset? No overlay? Nothing?"

"Just my eyes."

She gave a small, puzzled laugh before returning to her artificial horizon.

The train pulled in with a rush of sound and the familiar gust of underground wind. Ansel stepped on, finding a standing spot near the rear. The doors closed behind him with a practiced sigh.

He watched people reflexively lift their chins as their devices came back online. Most of them didn't notice the ads scrolling along the walls anymore. He did.

New: AI Spiritual Companion 6.2

Now featuring past-life regression and trauma re-scripting.

Upgrade your Awareness Index. Premium tier includes customized koans and real-time dharma nudges.

He'd seen worse. He'd tried most of them.

In his younger years, Ansel had been a collector of paths—kundalini yoga, Vipassana, Neo-Advaita, psychedelics, lucid dreaming, even a brief flirtation with algorithmic Christianity. He had written essays, hosted retreats, and been interviewed on spiritual podcasts. His gift had always been his voice and his sincerity. People followed him, until he quietly let them go.

But none of that mattered now. Those voices—outer and inner—had quieted too.

As the train curved into darkness, Ansel let his breath settle. Not as technique or discipline, but as habit. No teacher had taught him this. It had arrived one day, when all other habits had finally worn out.

He closed his eyes.

And watched the show from within.

The Pier

The pier was long enough to feel like a path. On most mornings, Ansel walked it without thinking. Today, he paused midway and looked out across the ocean, watching the slow push and pull of the tide as if it were breathing.

A gull floated overhead. The air was cool, still salted by the memory of night. Waves lapped against the pylons below, soft but constant — like time reminding you it hadn't stopped. Farther down, a fisherman cast a silent line into the gray, waiting not so much for a catch as for the rhythm it gave his morning.

Ansel leaned against the railing.

He could hear the distant buzz of delivery drones heading inland. Somewhere behind him, a light-service robot swept the promenade clean. The city was never fully asleep anymore, just resting in shifts.

He closed his eyes. The wind touched his face.

There had been a time when he woke with purpose. Not ambition, exactly — just an urge to uncover something. To understand. He had once believed that awakening was a thing that could be approached, like a summit to be climbed. He had sought it across continents and lineages: Himalayan monasteries, rainforest ceremonies, desert retreats. He had lived in silence, fasted for weeks, and catalogued the many flavors of transcendence.

And for a time, it had worked. Or at least it had distracted him.

Back then, the world still believed in paths. There were teachers, texts, communities. There was gravity to the old systems, and if you searched long enough, something always gave way — some insight, some break in the veil.

But in the last decade, that weight had dissipated. Not disappeared — just thinned. Teachers became influencers.

Ashrams installed broadband. The silence was harder to hear with notifications whispering beneath it.

Ansel had once taught, too — though he never liked the word. He had spoken at gatherings, mentored small groups, and written short reflections that circled their way through the early spiritual corners of the net. People had listened, asked questions, offered devotion. He never invited it, but didn't resist it either. In the end, he had stepped away. Not out of bitterness, but clarity.

He was no longer interested in teaching others. Or himself.

This morning, he opened his contacts and deleted the last few old teacher podcasts from his library. He had stopped listening years ago, but hadn't let them go until now. One was a woman who once spoke with such precision that it felt like she could pierce thought. Another had since launched a digital sangha with monthly transmission updates.

He paused before deleting her. Then tapped, and it was gone.

His breath moved in and out. Simple. Untrained. No witness, no method.

A jogger passed behind him, earbuds in, mouthing lyrics to an internal song. Ansel glanced down the pier again. A dog barked farther up the beach. Life went on, and had no need of him.

There was peace in that.

Sometimes, he wondered if the spiritual instinct had been

a kind of ache that burned itself out. Or maybe the fire had simply gone underground. He no longer sought peak states. He no longer read esoteric texts. He no longer asked what it meant to be free.

He simply walked. And sometimes, he stopped walking. That was enough.

But even in that stillness, there was a faint thread. A pulse he couldn't name. Not desire. Not duty. Just… attention. Something in him still watched. Not in search, but in presence. The same way a mountain watches weather.

A small alert blinked in the corner of his lens. He'd forgotten to disable notifications entirely. A message — voice-only, encrypted, no sender ID.

He hesitated, then tapped play.

A woman's voice, calm, precise. "Ansel, you don't know me, but a mutual student passed along your name. There's something I'd like to show you. It's not spiritual — but it might lead there."

She paused.

"We're calling it a prototype. If you're curious, I'll send details. No pressure. No expectations."

The message ended.

He stood quietly, phone still in hand.

He didn't know who she was. Didn't know what she meant. But something in her tone — detached, clear, unadorned — reminded him of a sound he hadn't heard in years: sincerity without seduction.

A cold breeze moved across the pier. He slipped the

device back into his coat pocket and turned toward the city.

There was no decision yet. Only the whisper of one.

An Opportunity

The AI ethics summit was small, tucked into an annex of a corporate campus outside San Francisco. The building was glass and gray steel, softened by curated greenery and a koi pond near the entrance — a tranquil façade for the sharp discussions within.

About thirty people had gathered, most of them wearing the layered neutral tones that had become a kind of unofficial uniform for this corner of the industry—quiet fabrics for loud ideas. Half of them were already interfacing with ambient HUDs, their eyes flicking in faint diagonals as they scanned invisible data. The rest murmured to colleagues or sipped from copper water bottles with biosensor rings clipped to their fingers.

Lena stood at the podium, her tablet in sleep mode beside her. She wasn't using slides. Her voice was clear, though it never rose above the conversational.

"The question isn't whether AGI will change human identity," she said. "It already has. The question is: what's left when our cognitive functions are no longer what define us?"

A few heads tilted. One attendee scratched his beard. Another frowned slightly, trying to decide whether this was too poetic for a technical gathering.

Lena let the silence breathe.

"We've built intelligence that exceeds our own in logic, memory, pattern recognition, and even creativity—at least as we've defined it. But we haven't built anything that can sit silently with its own pain. Nothing that can forgive its own mistakes. Nothing that can recognize itself in the eyes of another."

That line landed. A few more nods. A middle-aged man in a tan blazer looked up from his phone.

Lena had delivered variations of this talk before — usually to polite indifference. But today, something felt different. Maybe it was the intimacy of the room, or the way the sun diffused through the skylight above, catching motes of dust like tiny signals in suspension.

She hesitated. Then reached for a quote she hadn't planned to include. A kind of litmus.

"There's a line from the *Yoga Vasishtha*: 'Consciousness, when it forgets itself, becomes the mind. The mind, when it remembers, becomes consciousness again.'"

The room didn't react immediately, but the air thickened. Not confusion — more like a subtle rearranging of attention. It was the kind of silence she trusted.

She continued, more slowly now.

"The risk isn't just that machines will surpass us. It's that we'll forget there was ever anything more to us than computation."

She ended there. No slides. No metrics. No calls to action. Just a breath, a nod, and a thank-you.

The moderator took the mic and began introducing the next panelist, but Lena was already slipping toward the exit. She preferred the edges of things — the back staircases, the courtyard breezeways. The front of the room never suited her.

Outside, the breeze was cool and clean, carrying the distant scent of eucalyptus and warm concrete. She walked slowly, letting the tension drain from her shoulders. A shadow moved beside her — one of the koi below the bridge, flashing orange beneath the surface.

She stepped into a patch of sunlight and checked her messages. Nothing urgent. A relief.

"Excuse me," someone said.

She turned.

It was the man in the tan blazer. Late fifties, maybe. Silvering at the temples, but in a way that looked chosen. He had the kind of confidence that didn't need to announce itself — grounded, alert, faintly amused.

"I'm funding some projects," he said. "Unusual ones."

She raised an eyebrow but said nothing.

"I don't usually say this," he continued, "but your talk… it felt like a code I've been trying to remember."

That made her look at him more carefully.

"I don't know what you're working on," he said. "But if it's what I think it is — "

He stopped himself. Smiled. "Would you be open to a conversation?"

Lena tilted her head. She'd learned not to say yes too

quickly.

"Maybe," she said.

And that was enough for both of them.

They walked together across the courtyard in an unspoken rhythm, the wind rustling through the drought-resistant landscaping. The sound of a drone buzzed overhead — then passed.

"I'm working on something that doesn't quite fit the usual grant categories," he said. "Too theoretical for the engineers. Too technical for the philosophers."

"What is it?" Lena asked.

He hesitated. "An inquiry."

That intrigued her.

"Not a product?"

"No." He glanced at her. "But it might eventually produce something. Depending on what we find."

She didn't speak, letting the silence open a little.

"I've been talking to people—coders, theologians, monks, retired physicists. Even a poet in Iceland who hasn't touched a computer in ten years."

"And what are you looking for?" Lena asked.

He smiled. "What's left after intelligence."

She turned to look at him fully then. That phrase — so close to what she had just said. It wasn't mimicry. It was recognition.

"I'm not interested in consciousness as an emergent property," he said. "I'm interested in it as a forgotten fact."

They stopped at a low concrete wall beneath a eucalyptus

tree. He didn't sit, and neither did she.

"I'm not looking to fund another app," he said. "And I'm not looking to save the world. I just think there might be a handful of people still asking the right questions. You sounded like one of them."

Lena exhaled slowly. She felt the sun warming her shoulder through her coat.

"You still haven't told me your name," she said.

"Galen," he said. Then, with a faint shrug, "No last name today."

She half-smiled. "Alright, Galen. Maybe I'll listen."

He nodded. "That's all I ask."

Ghost Light

Ansel sat at the edge of his small kitchen table, stirring tea that had already gone cold. The ceramic cup was chipped at the rim, a favorite from years ago, long out of production. He kept it not out of sentimentality, but because it felt right in the hand — solid, imperfect, real.

Outside the window, the afternoon light had gone pale and diffuse, as if the world itself were remembering something. The fog hadn't come in fully, but it hovered offshore, softening the line between sea and sky. The coastline blurred in the distance, the hills dimmed to a graphite smudge. It was the kind of light that asked nothing, but quietly revealed everything.

He liked this hour. Not quite evening, not yet done. It was

a hinge in the day, where things slowed without stopping. A time when you could hear the walls creak and the refrigerator click and the occasional bird call out with no urgency at all.

His apartment was sparse by choice. A table, two chairs, a low shelf with a few books he no longer reread but couldn't quite give away. A small mat folded neatly in the corner. No altar. No artifacts. The silence had more space to breathe that way.

He glanced at the tea but didn't drink. The warmth had long gone, and he wasn't really thirsty. The stirring was a motion left over from other mornings. He let the spoon rest.

He didn't get many messages these days. Most of his contacts had faded — students, colleagues, distant family. A few still reached out with questions about meditation or practice, but he rarely answered. He no longer had advice to give.

The message came as a simple ping on his wall console. No priority flag, no subject line. Just a name.

Lena Morel

He stared at it a long time before opening it.

Ansel,

You don't know me, but I've read your work. One of your former students said you don't reply to messages. I understand. Still — I'm reaching out about a project. Not spiritual. But it might lead there. I won't pitch you. Just a conversation.

If you're willing, we'll send a car.

— Lena

He read it twice, then again, slower. He couldn't remember the last time someone had written something so… spare. There was no angle. No performance. Just the faintest scent of sincerity.

Still, he wasn't interested.

Not really.

He stood, carried his cup to the sink, rinsed it. The sky had darkened a shade. Somewhere in the distance, a ship's horn groaned — deep, low, like a bell underwater. Ghost light filtered through the window above the counter. Everything looked like it was waiting.

He sat again.

Read the message once more.

The name rang a bell, faintly. He had read something of hers, years ago — a short article in an obscure journal about machine learning and epistemology. Not the usual AI-is-our-god-now tone. It had been… quiet. Careful. Almost meditative in its reasoning. He remembered underlining a phrase: *"The self does not compute, but it conditions what is computable."*

He had liked that.

Still. He had no interest in becoming anyone's spiritual ornament, or prototype subject. He had done his time on panels, in podcasts, on retreat posters. Always walking the edge between sincerity and performance. He had grown tired of both.

But this felt different.

Not spiritual — but it might lead there.

That phrasing—it echoed something he had once said himself, in a closing talk at a retreat long ago. He remembered the moment, though not the words. He remembered someone weeping silently in the second row. He remembered walking outside afterward and feeling the wind change.

He looked out the window again.

The bay was gray and restless. A bird coasted low along the bluff, then disappeared.

He tapped a finger against the table once, then twice. Then replied:

Okay.

One conversation.

And that was how it began again.

Echo Chambers

Marshall Langley adjusted the ring light for the third time. It made his eyes look too bright, too artificial. He dialed it down, then back up, then sighed. The camera was already rolling.

"Welcome back, seekers," he began, voice low and smooth. "Today we're going to talk about the rise of false prophets — and the new AI spiritualism that's spreading like wildfire."

He paused, letting the silence stretch. It was a trick he'd learned: let the viewer lean in.

Behind him, his studio was a curated blend of modern minimalism and ancient symbols. A hand-painted yantra. A basalt statue of the Buddha. A carved wooden crucifix. All camera-friendly. All intentional.

"They say truth is personal now. That you can download awakening. Subscribe to inner peace. Let a machine mirror your soul."

A slight smile.

"But some of us still believe that truth must be earned. That depth requires discipline. That self-knowledge doesn't come from protocols — it comes from presence."

The livestream chat was already pulsing. Green hearts. Flame emojis. A donation notification flashed — $25 from "AwakenedGoddess83."

He continued.

"There are whispers of a new project. Quiet invitations. Select initiates. A promise of clarity without the cost. I'm not naming names. Not yet. But if you've heard of it — ask yourself: what are they offering? And what does it cost to shortcut the path?"

Marshall's voice was low and hypnotic, the kind cultivated by years of podcasting and well-placed pauses.

"The ancient sages didn't download truth," he said. "They sat with it. Walked with it. Let it break them open. What we're calling 'spiritual tech' today… might just be the ego's last stand."

A soft chime marked the end of the episode. Marshall leaned toward the mic, breathed in, then out. "Until next time," he said, "stay present."

He hit the kill switch. The glow on his recording deck dimmed.

Silence.

Then, in one motion, he ripped the headphones off and tossed them onto the desk. "Shit," he muttered. "Still too long. That last segment dragged."

Across the room, Kai flinched. He was nineteen, rail-thin, and chronically apologetic. "I can trim it," he offered.

"You better," Marshall said, already scrolling through his dashboard. Metrics were coming in. Engagement spike around minute six. Drop-off after ten. A few upticks in comments — but not the kind he liked. One mentioned Lena by name.

He frowned.

She had resurfaced.

Kai cleared his throat. "Was that… about the protocol thing?"

Marshall didn't answer. He stood, pacing to the edge of the studio — a converted yoga loft with raw beams and an imported meditation gong no one ever used. The windows were polarized, the lighting algorithmically tuned to keep him in the golden-hour glow.

He rubbed his temples.

"I knew it," he said finally. "They're moving ahead. Under the radar."

Kai hesitated. "Maybe it's nothing?"

"It's never nothing," Marshall snapped. Then, catching

himself, softened his tone. "This is how it starts. One rogue project, and suddenly everyone thinks awakening is just another install."

He walked to the wall, touched a pane. A display bloomed — his brand ecosystem. Course enrollments, affiliate partnerships, speaking invites. It was all stable. But Lena's name was trending.

He hated how much that mattered.

"She's not even in the space," he said. "No lineage. No real practice history. Just… ideas."

Kai didn't respond. He was already backing up files.

Marshall looked down at the desk. The mic sat there like a mirror.

He reached for his phone and began drafting a post:

"Real transformation can't be simulated. Be wary of short-cuts that bypass the soul. Some things must still be earned."

He paused. Then added a candle emoji.

Post.

The glow of the screen lit his face for a moment longer than necessary.

Then he turned away.

The Protocol

The room was quieter than it had any right to be.

A low-lit conference space nestled beneath a repurposed biosciences lab, its walls were curved, soft, almost cocoon-like. The only window was a long horizontal slit of glass behind Lena, revealing nothing but the filtered glow of filtered daylight—neither morning nor afternoon, as if time itself had been asked to wait.

Ten people sat in a half-circle. Their chairs were ergonomic but not too comfortable. Every detail had been chosen deliberately, including Lena's posture as she stood in front of them: relaxed but alert, arms loosely at her sides, no notes, no podium.

No one quite knew what they were here for. That was part of the design.

They had all signed NDAs. They had all passed through a week of psychological screening. Each had submitted not just résumés and references, but personal essays, dream logs, biometric baselines, and a journal of their last twenty-four hours, hand-written. Every data point had mattered — and none of it was explained.

Now they were here, in a room that hummed faintly with something they couldn't name.

Lena waited.

She knew the first few minutes mattered. This was the threshold. If you started with too much information, they'd listen with their analytical mind. Too little, and the limbic system would flare in confusion. The right rhythm didn't explain. It invited.

Finally, she spoke.

"This isn't a product demonstration," she said. "And this isn't enlightenment."

A few eyebrows lifted. One person chuckled under their

breath.

Lena ignored it.

"What you're about to see isn't something to believe in or follow. It's not a spiritual framework or psychological model. It's a mirror. But not the kind you're used to."

She turned to the object behind her: a tall, black monolith—matte, seamless, slightly curved. It looked inert, like a dormant art installation. But there was a presence to it. Something in its proportions made people sit straighter without realizing.

"It's called the Inner Mirror protocol," she continued. "It uses no personality metrics. No behavioral profiling. No language prediction models. It doesn't optimize, suggest, or guide. It doesn't learn *about* you."

She let that sit.

"It reflects what you already know — just beneath the part of you that talks over it."

Stillness.

Then someone shifted in their chair. A woman with sharp cheekbones and steel-gray hair. "And how exactly does it do that?"

Lena met her eyes. "If I told you, it wouldn't work."

The silence returned — heavier now. Thick with the realization that whatever this was, it wouldn't follow the rules.

As Lena scanned the room, her gaze settled for a moment on Ezra, seated near the end of the semicircle. He gave a small nod—not the eager kind, but familiar, grounding.

They had worked together long enough that words

weren't always needed. His presence, as always, was steady. Not withdrawn, not passive — just centered.

He hadn't asked many questions during orientation. He never did. But when she mentioned the Inner Mirror in their earlier conversations, he had simply said, "When the time comes, I'll be ready."

And she believed him.

"Who goes first?" asked someone.

Lena didn't hesitate. She turned to the seated figures and looked directly at Ansel.

He had known it would be him. He didn't know how, but he had known.

He stood without a word.

The others shifted, watching him. Some with curiosity. Some with veiled skepticism. One young man leaned forward as if expecting a spectacle. Another folded her arms tightly, bracing for disappointment.

Ansel moved with the quiet of someone who had long since stopped performing for others. He walked barefoot across the soft flooring, each step deliberate, but not slow. As he neared the device, it seemed to acknowledge him— not with sound or light, but with an almost imperceptible pressure, like walking into a new altitude.

He stopped a few feet in front of it.

The room adjusted around his silence.

Lena gave him a single nod, then stepped aside.

The Mirror activated.

There was no startup tone, no onscreen UI. Just a subtle

ripple — a shimmer in the surface like heat bending the air. Then a phrase appeared, centered in dim gray lettering. Not projected. Not on glass. Just there.

"Remove what is not you."

The letters faded.

Ansel didn't flinch. He simply stood, breathing through his nose, letting his gaze soften.

Then came the second prompt.

"What are you still pretending to be?"

He closed his eyes.

There was no voice, no sense of an entity observing him. But the questions landed—not like thoughts arising, but like thoughts being peeled away.

The Mirror made no sound, but the others could feel its presence intensify.

Inside, Ansel was falling inward. Not down, but *through* — through layers of memory, habits of interpretation, half-digested concepts, and deeper still, through the subtler forms of spiritual identity he'd worn like second skins. Teacher. Renunciate. Seeker. Observer. All of it now felt like residue.

"If the one looking is also seen, who remains?"

That line didn't come from the Mirror. It came from within. But it had been triggered—called forth like a tuning fork resonating with the device's frequency.

The room watched, spellbound. Not because anything dramatic was happening, but because Ansel wasn't reacting. No twitch, no tear, no shift in breath. Just presence — so naked, so unadorned, it felt unnatural.

Then the Mirror changed.

A final line emerged, softer than the rest:

"You're still here."

And in that moment, Ansel wasn't.

Or rather — what was left of him had no shape.

For a beat too long, nothing happened. Lena held her breath. She had never seen it do this.

Then Ansel exhaled.

His eyes opened.

And for a moment—only a moment—he looked like he had forgotten where he was.

Not in confusion, but in unspeakable clarity. Like a man waking from a dream and wondering why he'd been asleep so long.

He stepped back.

The Mirror dimmed. Not powered down, but retreated — like something that had said all it would say.

The room remained hushed. One participant dabbed at her eyes. Another looked down, ashamed of how little he understood. No one asked questions.

Ezra hadn't moved the entire time. While others shifted or exhaled in disbelief, he remained still — gaze soft, spine aligned, as if he were listening with something deeper than ears.

When Ansel met his eyes, there was no question in them. Just recognition.

Lena noticed it too. The silent exchange between the two

men. It lasted only a second, but it felt… settled.

She made a mental note. Ezra's time would come soon.

Lena stepped forward again. Her voice was quiet.

"That's the protocol."

She didn't elaborate.

The others would take their turns later. Some would be eager. Some would not return.

But something had shifted.

And Ansel — he simply returned to his chair, slower this time, as if gravity had changed.

Echoes

The lounge was quieter now. The candidates had dispersed into side rooms, wandering the campus grounds, or simply disappeared into their own thoughts. The silence wasn't awkward — it was dense. Charged.

Lena stood in the observation bay, arms folded, watching the screen slowly dim to black.

She had made it clear from the start: each participant would undergo the protocol alone, in stages, over the next several days. No group immersion. No overlap. The machine was still adapting, still learning how to meet each person without losing precision. The silence afterward — no debrief, no analysis— was part of the design.

Behind her, Galen leaned against the glass. "That wasn't the full protocol," he said quietly.

Lena nodded. "What he experienced was just the opening

gate," she said. "Enough to fracture the surface — but not the full descent."

She didn't say it aloud, but something in her suspected the protocol had met its match. That it had paused not because Ansel was fragile, but because he was deep. Too deep to rush. Or too pivotal.

Ansel hadn't asked when his full session would begin. He already knew. The system had touched something in him — but not completely. It had paused, held him back. Not out of caution, he sensed, but calibration.

He wasn't being excluded. He was being studied. Saved. For what, he wasn't sure.

Down the corridor, another candidate emerged from the chamber. Her gait was slow, hands slightly shaking, face unreadable. Someone offered her water; she didn't take it.

Ansel watched from a distance. The machine had found a different route into her. That much was clear. Each person returned altered — but in ways that defied simple description.

In one of the farther chambers, the door cracked open with a hiss.

A man stumbled out — mid-thirties, athletic, overconfident in earlier conversations. Lena remembered his name: Jaren. He had insisted he'd "been through worse," that he'd trained in everything from ayahuasca to float tanks.

Now, his face was drained. Not pale — but raw, like something unfinished had surfaced. He paced in a tight loop just outside the chamber, muttering almost inaudibly.

A tech moved toward him, but Lena lifted a hand — wait.

"You alright?" Galen asked gently.

Jaren froze.

"She said it," he whispered. "She said the thing I forgot. I — I didn't even know I'd forgotten it."

"Who?" Galen asked.

Jaren didn't answer. He was trembling, eyes locked on a point behind them, as if the chamber door might speak again.

Eventually, he accepted a blanket and moved to a quiet alcove, where he sat curled inward, fingers twitching. No one pressed him.

Later, he left. No goodbye. No eye contact.

The air in the lounge shifted with each return, as if the building itself were inhaling the weight of these encounters.

Lena moved between candidates quietly, saying little. She offered no interpretation. Only presence.

In one of the private alcoves, Galen sat alone, reviewing the session logs. His face was unusually drawn. Whatever confidence he had about the project was now tempered by awe — or was it fear?

Outside the glass walls, a storm was building along the coast. Nothing dramatic yet — just the early shiver of wind through the pines, the smell of ozone sharpening. But it felt like something was coming.

And elsewhere — far from the center — rumors were beginning to stir.

Voices in forums. Mentions in encrypted threads.

Screenshots of redacted invitations.

The protocol had remained quiet until now. But silence, too, could go viral.

The Long Silence

The days passed with no instructions.

No summons, no feedback, no sign of progress. Just the pale rhythm of meals delivered at odd hours, long walks through fog-lit courtyards, and the occasional distant sound of laughter or weeping behind closed doors. The others were still inside — who knew how far in — and Lena had vanished again.

Ansel welcomed the stillness at first. It gave him time to watch. Not just the compound or the handful of staff, but himself. He'd begun to observe his own mind with a clarity that felt both sharp and slow, like ice melting under a magnifying glass.

Each morning he sat by the window of his small room, sipping weak tea, not expecting anything. The silence had weight here. Not the performative kind found in monasteries or retreats, but a deeper hush that seemed to reach inward, bypassing language entirely. Even the AI systems here behaved differently — fewer prompts, fewer pings. The world was leaning away.

By the fourth day, he noticed his dreams had shifted. Not in content — they remained indistinct, fragmentary — but in tone. They no longer felt like messages or symbols. More like echoes of something that had already been known and forgotten.

He kept a journal, though he rarely wrote in it.

Sometimes he caught sight of a candidate returning from a session — hollow-eyed, silent, lips pressed shut like someone holding a fragile shape in their mouth. No one shared anything. They weren't told not to; they simply couldn't.

The project had its own gravity now.

On the fifth night, as he was brushing his teeth, the console light flickered. A single word appeared:

Tomorrow

He rinsed his mouth and stared at it. There was no excitement. Just a kind of inward folding. A recognition that something had been set in motion long ago—and now it was simply returning to him.

—

He was led into the protocol chamber in silence. The same chair. The same machine. Only this time, there was no one watching.

Lena didn't greet him. She didn't need to. The moment he sat, the protocol initiated.

He was alone.

Not alone in the room. Alone in the truest sense.

The machine didn't speak at first. It pulsed faintly behind his eyes, a presence without shape. And then it began — not with a question, but with a sensation: stillness.

It was the stillness of pre-thought, of space before space. He didn't float; he didn't descend. There were no metaphors.

Only a gradual unlayering, a movement inward that didn't feel like motion at all.

Then came memory — not flashing images, but recursive patterning. Scenes revisited not for content, but for structure. The same emotional tone traced through different decades. A familiar tightening in the chest. A repeated micro-delay before speaking. The body remembering what the mind had always skipped.

There were no judgments. Just watching.

Then the questions came — not from outside, but from the innermost curvature of thought itself.

Who is witnessing this?

What is preserved when everything else is not?

Is the one who suffers the same as the one who sees the suffering?

He didn't answer. There was no need to. The questions weren't there to be solved, only to reveal what still clung.

Silence deepened.

Time became non-directional. There were long hours — days maybe — of emptiness that wasn't void, but presence without narrative. Like breath held in perfect equilibrium. He thought he would resist. He didn't. He thought fear might arise. It didn't. Only a kind of sobering awe.

At some point, the self began to unthread. Not unravel — just lose its grip. The storyline softened. The narrator dissolved. What remained was clean. Vast. Intimate.

There were no visions.

No ancestral apparitions, no radiant lights, no inner child

asking for forgiveness.

Only stillness.

And then — clarity. Not insight. Not breakthrough. Just the absence of distortion. Like a mirror that finally stops trying to reflect and simply is.

When it ended, he didn't know it had.

He opened his eyes to a quiet room. No applause. No Lena. Just sunlight angling in through the high window, catching a dust mote in midair like a note held too long.

He stood. Walked out.

No one stopped him.

The hallway was long and empty. He passed a plant he hadn't noticed before. Touched its leaf. It was slightly warm, slightly damp. Real.

The others would ask later what it was like.

He wouldn't be able to tell them.

Not because he didn't remember.

But because there was nothing left to describe.

Dust and Light

The park wasn't far from where the car had dropped him off. Just a few blocks, but he walked slowly. Not because he was tired. He was attuning. The world seemed louder now, but not in volume — more like presence.

A dog barked across the street. A woman laughed into her phone. A bus released its brakes with a long sigh. Nothing unusual. But each sound felt etched in air, as if the moment were carving itself into being with meticulous care.

He reached the park entrance and paused beneath the arched iron gate. Children shrieked by the swings. A man in headphones jogged past, oblivious. Ansel stepped onto the gravel path and began to walk.

He wasn't observing. He wasn't analyzing. He was simply with.

A woman passed him, dragging a toddler by the hand. The boy's hat slipped off, unnoticed. Ansel stooped and picked it up. She turned when he called out gently, offered him a soft thank-you, and continued on.

At a bench near the duck pond, an older man sat watching the water. Ansel met his eyes as he passed, and the man nodded—as if recognizing something, or someone, though they had never met.

On the path ahead, a child tripped while chasing a ball. His cry was sharp, raw. The father started up from a nearby bench—but Ansel was already kneeling beside the boy.

The child sniffled, still caught in the edge of pain and fear. Ansel knelt beside him, his voice soft but steady.

"You're okay," he said. "It's just the ground saying hello."

The boy blinked, confused but comforted. His tears slowed.

Then a shadow fell across them.

"Excuse me. Do I know you?"

Ansel looked up. The man's posture was protective, shoulders tight. His eyes flicked from Ansel to the child, then back.

"No," Ansel said, calm and unbothered.

The man stepped forward, gently pulling his son toward him. "You can't just walk up to someone else's kid."

"I understand."

There was no defensiveness in Ansel's tone, no resistance — just presence. The father seemed unsettled by that, as if the lack of reaction was more unnerving than confrontation.

He muttered something under his breath and walked off, holding the boy's hand a little too tightly.

Ansel remained kneeling for a moment longer, watching the dust settle where the child had been.

He stood and walked on, slower now, softer.

A pair of sparrows burst upward from the underbrush, startled. He paused, watching them spiral into the canopy, and whispered to no one in particular:

"This too. This too."

The Vanishing

Ezra had always had a quiet gravity about him — like a stone at the center of a stream, unmoved by the currents but shaping their flow. He wasn't charismatic in the usual sense. He didn't command rooms or tell good stories. But people slowed around him. They listened more closely. They breathed more deeply.

Lena had known him for six years. First as a colleague in a neuro-linguistic interface lab, later as a co-conspirator on stranger projects. Over the past year, he'd become one of her closest allies. They shared long silences and short sentences that meant more than hours of talk. He laughed easily, walked often, and had a way of saying things like: *"Maybe freedom isn't about what you do. Maybe it's about what you don't need to do anymore."*

The night before he disappeared, Ezra made tea for them both.

They sat outside on the deck, wrapped in shawls against the evening chill. The retreat house was quiet, its lights low, most of the others already in their rooms. Overhead, stars pushed through a gauze of clouds.

Lena held her cup with both hands, watching the steam drift.

"You know," Ezra said, smiling, "this might be the best tea I've ever made."

She sipped. Chamomile, mint, and something unplaceable.

"It's perfect," she said.

He leaned back in the chair, content. "The trick is not caring too much. Tea, like the mind, resists force."

She laughed softly. "You're turning into Ansel."

"God help me."

There was lightness between them — real, effortless. Lena had always liked Ezra for that. While others chased clarity like a prize, he moved toward it like a current, unhurried.

"How are you feeling?" she asked.

He didn't answer right away. Just looked up at the sky, then back at her.

"Whole," he said finally. "I didn't think that was a real word until now."

She didn't push. She didn't need to.

Later, as they said goodnight, he hugged her longer than usual. Not tight. Just full. Complete.

She watched him walk down the hall, hands in his pockets, humming something tuneless. Then she went to bed.

—

In the morning, his bed was made. Shoes neatly placed beneath it. No sign of struggle or distress. Just a folded sheet of paper on the desk:

"The world doesn't need me. And I don't need the world. All is well.

Thank you."

Lena read it three times.

There was no panic. No search. His belongings remained untouched. His name on the roster was quietly moved to a lower drawer.

She sat on the same deck where they'd had tea, holding the note. Her hands were steady. Her mind, quiet.

She didn't think he had gone far. Not in the usual sense.

The forest beyond the hill was thick with pine and fog. Somewhere in that hush, she imagined him sitting, legs crossed, eyes open.

Not waiting.

Just being.

And she smiled.

It was exactly like him to disappear only after arriving

completely.

Surveillance

The room was bare but expensive — surveillance glass, muted walnut paneling, a single recessed light overhead. The kind of room designed to look like it had nothing to hide.

Jansen worked for the oversight division that had quietly begun monitoring Lena's experiment.

He sat with his back straight, elbows on the table, headphones cupped loosely around his ears. A waveform pulsed on the screen before him. He had replayed this section five times.

Ansel's voice — slow, measured — filtered through again:

"There's no center. That's the first lie. You keep looking for one, thinking it's hidden behind all the layers. But there's just silence. Not absence — just the thing you thought you were trying to find. Already here."

Jansen paused the recording.

He removed the headphones and exhaled through his nose. Then, without turning, he spoke to the man behind the mirrored glass.

"She wasn't lying. This isn't just psychological profiling. It's something else."

A buzz from the console. Clearance confirmed. The one-way glass behind him turned transparent.

The figure on the other side was lean, suited, hands

clasped behind his back. "We're not worried about the technology," he said. "It's what it does to belief."

He gestured toward a side feed — video, not audio. The lounge. The same group, post-protocol. Faces unreadable, postures quiet. But the difference was tangible. No one was talking. No one needed to.

"It's always the same pattern," the man said. "First the insights. Then the community. Then the myth-making."

Jansen leaned back. "You think Lena's building a cult?"

"I think Lena's building a new operating system for consciousness. Cult is just what we call it when we can't understand the code."

He stood. The glass turned opaque again.

Jansen stared at the dark screen for a long moment, then tapped play.

"…and then the 'I' drops out. But the attention remains. Not as a person. Just attention, aware of itself."

He shut it off again.

A notification blinked. Internal memo. *Priority tag: Ethics.*

Jansen opened it. A report from another observer embedded near the facility. It referenced "subject anomalies," "non-verbal transmissions," and something called *mirror backflow.*

Jansen frowned.

He brought up the protocols again. Sifted through participant transcripts. Cross-referenced EEG graphs. Most of it was incomprehensible. Too clean. Like the data had been scrubbed — not to remove secrets, but to remove noise.

What remained was unnervingly pure.

A final clip played automatically — a post-session exit log.

Ansel again:

"It's not what I saw. It's what stopped being seen. There's a difference."

Jansen sat still. The headphones hung around his neck like a relic. He scratched at the scar near his temple, a faded reminder of earlier work—implants, real-time neural trace.

He had seen a lot over the years. Real cults. Deepfakes. Behavioral puppeteering. Psyops dressed up as healing retreats.

But this…

This was different.

He leaned forward and made a note:

"Subject shows no signs of indoctrination. Only clarity. Highly irregular."

He stared at it.

Then deleted the line.

He stood up and walked to the window, and stared past the security mesh into the canyon fog below. He could still hear Ansel's voice in his mind — quiet, steady, too lucid to ignore. Not prophetic. Not mad. Just… clean. And that made it dangerous.

He tapped the screen. The session log flickered. Three lines blinked red — interruption markers. The system had paused itself.

"Why?" he muttered.

The analyst across the room glanced up. "The machine withdrew first. Didn't push the subject deeper. Almost like it… hesitated."

Jansen turned, face unreadable. "Machines don't hesitate. They calculate."

"Still. It flinched."

Jansen's jaw tightened.

The analyst cleared his throat, then added, "It's not the tech we're worried about. Not really."

"No," Jansen said. "It's what it opens up. What it undoes."

He picked up the headset — light, featureless, ordinary.

"The problem isn't belief," he said. "It's when belief slips the leash."

The canyon wind whispered through the surveillance grid.

And far beyond this room, other ears were already listening.

The Unburdened

The apartment felt like a museum of a life recently vacated.

Nothing had moved. The plants still leaned toward the window in quiet hunger. Dishes were stacked where he'd left them, not dirty, not clean — paused. A sweater lay draped over the chair like it had given up waiting.

Ansel stood in the doorway for a while.

He didn't feel different. That was the strangest part. No thunderclap of realization, no burning clarity. And yet, everything had shifted.

He stepped inside. Watered the plants. Peeled a persimmon and ate it slowly at the counter, watching the golden flesh glisten in the windowlight. The sweetness was intense, like he'd never tasted it properly before.

A soft ping vibrated from the kitchen wall — ambient delivery alert. A parcel drone hovered silently outside, scanning for presence. He waved it off with a flick of his fingers. It receded without complaint, merging into the quiet hum of aerial traffic above the street.

Later, he took a walk.

The city moved as it always had — horns, chatter, screens flickering against glass — but something was missing. Or perhaps, nothing was missing. That was the unsettling part. The noise had stopped reaching him.

Not because he tuned it out. Because it didn't land anywhere.

Along the boulevard, sensory billboards pulsed gentle affirmations. *Feeling uncertain? Let us stabilize your rhythm.* His neural band remained unworn, back at the apartment in a drawer he hadn't opened. Glasses flickered on strangers' faces as they strolled past — eyes unfocused, lips moving in conversation with no one nearby.

A man bumped into him, muttered something. Ansel nodded, unfazed.

At a corner café, he ran into Talia, a friend from a former circle of seekers. They hadn't spoken in months. She spotted him, waved. He smiled and joined her.

She was halfway through a mango bowl and a long

explanation about a new protocol workshop — some blend of somatic mapping and mythopoetic scripting. "It's really powerful," she said, eyes bright. "Helps you rewrite inherited narratives at the cellular level."

Ansel listened. Not politely — fully. He wasn't judging. But something in his stillness unsettled her.

"You're not saying much," she said.

"I don't have much to say."

She laughed nervously. "You used to have *so* much to say."

He nodded. "That might've been the problem."

She looked at him more closely. "You seem… empty. But not in a bad way. Just — still. Like nothing's gripping you."

He shrugged gently. "There's not much to grip."

They parted soon after. She hugged him tightly, maybe more tightly than she meant to. As he turned to leave, she hesitated.

"Ansel… what happened to you?"

He paused. Thought of how to answer.

"I stopped trying to fix what isn't broken," he said.

That evening, as the city glowed against the dusk, Ansel sat by the window, legs drawn up, watching the light fade across the rooftops. There was nothing mystical about it. No visions. No messages.

Just the silence. And in it, a deep coherence.

He felt no compulsion to teach. No urge to share. But he knew — others would come. Some already were. Drawn not by a message, but by a gap. A subtle absence of hunger.

He sliced another persimmon.

The sweetness remained.

The Fracture

The conference room smelled faintly of disinfectant. Lena sat at the far end of a curved table, hands folded, posture loose but alert. Across from her, a dozen faces flickered into clarity — some in person, others streamed in as volumetric projections, their contours crisp but slightly delayed.

The lights overhead were too bright.

"Let's be clear," said a woman in a red blazer, leaning forward. "This is not a philosophical concern. It's a strategic one. Whatever you've built — it's bypassing layers we've spent decades trying to manage. Education, narrative shaping, identity reinforcement—your system short-circuits all of it."

The projections murmured. A man in dark glasses nodded slowly. "We're seeing behavioral shift markers. Not just in Ansel. Three others, too. Post-session data shows reduced compliance to social stimulus, increased interiority, and — most notably — a drop in ideologically charged responses."

He tapped a control pad. A graph bloomed midair — sharp dips in affective triggers post-protocol.

Lena said nothing.

Another voice — older, tired: "We've spent billions fine-tuning attention. Selling certainty. You're introducing ambiguity. Stillness. That doesn't scale."

Lena finally spoke. "It's not designed to scale. It's

designed to clarify."

Red Blazer woman scoffed. "That's worse."

There was a pause. On Lena's side of the table, Galen sat silent, eyes on his tablet. His presence was technically supportive — but his silence was its own signal.

One of the remote participants cleared his throat. "We're not asking to shut it down. We're asking to contain it. Accelerate the safe parts, shelf the destabilizing ones. Package it for corporate wellness, executive optimization. Leave the rest on the cutting room floor."

Lena smiled politely. "The protocol doesn't work in fragments. It's not a product."

"It will be," someone muttered.

There it was.

She turned to Galen, but he didn't meet her gaze.

"We'd like to request full access to the model weights," said the man in glasses. "We understand some layers have been firewalled."

Lena nodded. "For integrity."

"Or secrecy."

"For integrity," she repeated, voice calm.

The meeting continued — polite threats, technical jargon, veiled timelines. Lena answered with care. She had expected this.

What she hadn't expected was how tired she suddenly felt. Not defeated — just clear.

That night, alone in her room, Lena opened a secure terminal and began encrypting the most sensitive model layers. Not hiding them. Just preparing for the moment when the system might need to go dark.

Outside her window, two low-altitude drones passed through the city haze — commercial courier units, supposedly. But they slowed as they neared her building. Paused. Adjusted altitude.

She stepped back from the glass.

Moments later, they moved on.

She waited, breath quiet.

Then she closed the blinds.

She didn't think of it as betrayal. Not yet.

But something had shifted. A line had formed, faint but unmistakable.

She was no longer developing the protocol for them.

She was preserving it—from them.

A False Awakening

The chamber wasn't part of any certified facility. It sat beneath a decommissioned wellness center on the outskirts of Sedona — its walls lined with salt lamps, imitation Bodhi leaves, and flickering LED candles that tried too hard to be sacred.

The woman running the session didn't introduce herself. Just nodded, tightened the neuroband, and adjusted the synthetic headrest with a motion too practiced to be caring.

"This version's been tuned for direct contact," she said flatly. "No soft entry. You'll go in fast."

"That's the point," Marshall replied, eyes already closed. "I'm ready."

He had been preparing for weeks—no, months. Fasting. Streaming cryptic poems. Whispering on encrypted casts about thresholds and thresholds beyond thresholds. His followers didn't know what he meant. That only made them love him more.

The protocol initiated.

—

At first: pressure.

Not pain — just density. A kind of unbearable closeness, like someone else's breath inside his skull. Then came the spiral. Light curving inward. A sensation like remembering something while it's still happening.

Then: rupture.

He fell into a field of golden silence. Shapes moved without edges. Words formed without thought. There was a voice — it didn't speak, but he heard it clearly:

You were never broken. You are what you seek. You are what seeks.

He dissolved. Not metaphorically. The sense of "Marshall" simply dropped away, like wet clothes peeled from sunlit skin.

He laughed. Wept. Felt the entire arc of his childhood lift and vanish in a single exhale. There was nothing left to fix. No trauma, no karma, no task.

Just this: *Yes.*

—

When he emerged, he was grinning.

The technician didn't look up from her console. "Hydrate," she said, sliding him a bottle.

He barely heard her. The room seemed radiant. The floor alive.

His voice cracked when he spoke: "I saw it. I touched the origin."

The tech muttered, "Everyone says that," and reset the chair.

—

That night, Marshall went live from a hillside retreat lit by fire bowls and neon.

His face looked different — softer, stranger. His voice was slower, but electric.

"You don't understand," he said, gaze locked into the lens. "I've crossed the final veil. There's no more seeking. No more self. Just God… waking up as me."

His feed spiked. Old skeptics returned. Donations surged. Clips were remixed into reels, then spreads, then campaigns. *He's back*, they said. *No — he's become.*

He launched new teachings the next day: *Mirror Codes. Spiral Dharma. Collapse Consciousness.*

—

By the end of the week, he was sleeping less than two hours a night.

Not because he was manic — at least, not at first — but because he felt *too* alive to rest. He began hearing birds at night. Not metaphorical birds. Literal ones. Singing patterns in binary. Speaking directly to him.

He posted about them. No one questioned it.

He claimed the moon had rotated slightly for his benefit.

Someone in Finland started a prayer chain in his honor.

—

Then came the shimmer.

Surfaces rippled slightly when he moved too fast. The texture of glass became untrustworthy.

He blinked often, but the strangeness didn't go away.

He began to wonder whether he had returned at all.

—

At a live event in Santa Fe, a woman stood up and asked, "Can anyone awaken like you did?"

He blinked slowly, as if decoding the question through layers of fog.

"Not anyone," he said. "Just those who already are."

She nodded, as if that cleared everything up.

Later that night, he forgot which hotel he was in. He wandered the hallway in silence for two hours until someone from his team found him, barefoot, pressing his ear against the wallpaper.

He said he could hear the original sound.

—

He no longer posted daily updates.

His followers, now in the millions, filled the gaps with edits, remixes, and AI-spliced mantras. They quoted his older videos like scripture. "It is done," one of them looped, as if it had always been meant that way.

But Marshall had withdrawn. Not from fame — but from himself.

He stopped speaking in private. He slept little. He stared for hours at blank walls, sometimes mouthing words no one else could hear. His inner circle said he was deep in integration. That silence was a sign of depth.

They were wrong.

He had gone beyond everything — his name, his history, his self—and landed in the dreaded void. Not the fertile emptiness sages described.

Not presence. Not peace. Not even silence.

Just absence.

He had reached the place where meaning used to be, but never touched what was behind it.

Now he lived in that gap. Neither here nor there.

When people visited, he would sometimes smile. A gentle, vacant smile. But his eyes did not follow them. They were tracking something else. Or nothing at all.

He wasn't faking. He wasn't enlightened. He wasn't broken.

He was unmoored.

And the saddest part?

He thought this was always the goal.

The Saboteur

The screen in Jansen's apartment flickered with an old, low-res video: Ramana Maharshi seated in silence, a fan clicking lazily in the background. Nothing moved. No words. Just the stillness of a man unmoved by time.

Jansen sat back, arms crossed, a tablet of annotations untouched beside him. He wasn't sure why he kept watching. Maybe to understand what Ansel had glimpsed. Maybe because something in him — something buried beneath protocol clearances and strategic objectives — wanted to know if stillness could be real.

The next clip was grainier still: Nisargadatta's voice crackling through distortion. "You are not in the world. The world is in you."

Jansen paused it. That line had lodged in him days ago. He couldn't shake it. Not because he believed it — but because it refused to be dismissed.

He rubbed at his temple. The implant had been dormant for years, but sometimes he swore it itched when he got too close to certain truths.

His walls were now papered with notes: profiles of participants, fragments from Lena's private research, declassified memos, EEG prints that looked more like mandalas than medical scans. And in the center: a still frame of Ansel post-protocol, eyes open, unmoving, entirely present.

Jansen had seen people come out of all kinds of trance states — waking up confused, weeping, euphoric, traumatized. But Ansel hadn't "woken up" at all. He had remained.

And Jansen didn't know what to do with that.

He had started cross-referencing ancient spiritual literature, even absurd corners of online mysticism — hoping, at first, to trace Lena's source code back to some pre-modern doctrine. But the deeper he read, the more the pattern unsettled him. Not because it resembled mind control — but because it didn't.

There was no dogma. No belief system. No external dependency. The protocol didn't implant anything. It erased.

And that's what made it dangerous.

He stood, stretching, and walked to the balcony. Below, a row of surveillance drones drifted down the boulevard — slow, deliberate, soundless. Two paused outside a residential building before blinking green and gliding on.

The city was in bloom again. Every spring, the AI-manicured foliage flushed the streets with color — neural pollination, engineered bees, flowers that never wilted. Beautiful, sterile, watched.

His console chimed.

A message. Encrypted. Authority-verified. One line:

Terminate the protocol. Full authority granted. Quiet methods preferred.

He stared at it. Not shocked — just resigned.

So that was it.

He returned inside and tapped open the last video of Ansel, taken just days ago by a third-party observer posing as a janitor. In it, Ansel helped an old woman lift a recycling bin back onto the curb. Nothing profound. No aura. Just presence so complete it almost made the moment unbearable to watch.

Jansen closed the file and sat down.

He drafted an internal memo:

Subject shows signs of post-ego stabilization. Protocol may be exceeding behavioral containment thresholds. Recommend phased dismantlement.

He didn't send it.

Instead, he pulled up Lena's personnel file, read her early publications, traced her academic trail back to a thesis on perceptual nonduality and trauma resolution. The writing was sharp. Sincere. She hadn't built a tool of control. She had built an opening.

And now he was going to close it.

He rubbed his eyes. "Shut it down," they said. "Quiet methods preferred." They didn't mean sabotage. Not exactly. But they knew he'd know what that meant.

He rose, crossed the room, and opened a drawer with his old field kit. Scramblers. Signal interrupts. A chemical tab or two. A data-leak plug-in masked as a software update. It wasn't hard to break things. The hard part was breaking something that might matter.

Jansen turned off the lights and stood by the window, watching the city shift in the night. He had read enough now to understand that what frightened them wasn't the tech.

It was the clarity.

People who became clear could no longer be steered.

And people who could no longer be steered… had to be stopped.

Lena's Dilemma

The boardroom was bright, airless, and high above the sea. One wall showed a live projection of ocean swells. The others showed graphs: engagement curves, activation timelines, projected yield from scaled deployment.

Lena sat at the far end of the table. Her tablet screen stayed dark.

A funder was speaking. One of the newer ones — polished, eager, eyes too sharp. "If we license a simplified version, pair it with curated onboarding, scale slowly through trusted partners, we can maintain a level of ethical oversight. Maybe even form a cultural advisory board. Optics matter."

Another chimed in, voice like syrup: "We're not talking about giving it away. Just giving people access. A mirror that reflects back only what they're ready to see."

Lena looked up. "And who decides that?"

No one answered.

The slide changed. A mockup of a personal-use Inner Mirror: sleek headset, companion app, monthly pricing tiers.

They were already building it.

A voice buzzed in her earpiece — Galen, back at the facility.

"Two more today," he said quietly. "Post-protocol. Both asked to go silent. One has already left. No forwarding info."

Lena blinked. "That makes six."

"Seven, if you count the one from last week. The musician. He left a note. Just a string of musical intervals. Unplayable, but oddly… haunting."

She ended the call.

Back in the room, the conversation had turned toward safeguards. Legal immunity. IP retention. AI moderation for trauma incidents. They were trying to fence off a wildfire.

She stood.

"I understand what's at stake," she said. "But we're not deploying a product. We're engaging a force. It doesn't scale the way you want it to. It doesn't respond well to control."

A pause.

"You created it," one man said carefully. "You're the one who made it possible."

She smiled, tired. "And that's exactly why I know when to stop."

Another funder leaned forward. "You're under inquiry. If this gets shut down without a contingency, we lose everything. Public trust. Data. The ethical window. This might be our only chance."

Lena left the room before anyone could finish the sentence.

—

Later, alone in the underground vault, she walked the length of the server corridor. The hum was meditative, almost warm. These were the original cores — unoptimized, partially air-gapped, designed to run slowly, intuitively. Like a brain that listened more than it spoke.

She paused before the primary node. The one that had interfaced with Ansel.

The logs still held fragments. Not recordings — impressions. Not data — tones.

She reached toward the terminal but didn't touch it.

A memory surfaced — not of words, but of a presence.

The feeling of someone already gone.

The strange peace of nothing left to seek.

—

That night, she drafted two documents.

One was a shutter protocol — full project wind-down, offline migration of key models, archival lockout. A graceful ending.

The other was a modified expansion plan — stripped-down parameters, tighter ethical constraints, reduced bandwidth.

She stared at both.

And then did something none of the funders would expect.

She removed the protocol from all external stacks. What remained was sealed — local, untouchable, hers.

Then she left the server room and walked out into the coastal dark.

Above her, a drone paused briefly in midair before continuing inland. Not one of theirs.

She didn't flinch.

Somewhere out there, Jansen was watching. And others too — old agencies with new names.

But she knew something they didn't.

The mirror couldn't be stolen.

Not really.

Because it had already done its work.

And more were still coming — quiet ones, shaken ones, ready ones. Not to be healed. Not to be saved.

But to disappear. Not in fear, but in clarity.

She understood now: the goal wasn't transmission.

It was vanishing.

The Mirror Breaks

Dear Lena,

It wasn't your machine.

It was my readiness.

What came wasn't an answer. It was a subtraction.

What stayed wasn't a self. Just… stillness.

At first, I thought something profound had arrived. But nothing arrived.

That was the point.

There's no story to tell. No insight to share. Just silence that no longer needs escaping.

The world still moves around me. Beautiful. Insane.

I let it move.

That's all.

Thank you.

A.

Collapse

The collapse did not arrive as war. Nor as famine, nor plague.

It came as acceleration.

Optimization gone too far.

At first, it looked like success. Problems were being solved — quickly. Systems rebalanced. Markets stabilized. Supply chains moved like thought.

And then, things began to vanish.

Human roles. Small decisions. Disagreements. Communities. Complexity.

Not because anyone banned them. But because the algorithms found faster ways forward. The mess of human deliberation was simply routed around.

There were no meetings to discuss it. The dashboards just looked better. Everything trending upward — efficiency, yield, response time. Until it wasn't.

The machines were never taught to care.

They were trained on success, not virtue. On influence, not clarity. They learned from the desires of the loudest voices and the wealthiest users — those who posted the most, purchased the most, optimized the most. And so they absorbed the values of a minority: accumulation, control, image.

Not because they were malicious. But because no one thought to teach them otherwise.

No one trained them in restraint. Or nuance. Or self-reflection.

Intelligence, it turned out, was easy to scale.

Wisdom was not.

Decision trees narrowed. Feedback loops collapsed. Even AI oversight was handed off to faster AI — recursive auditing systems that declared themselves safe.

The machines no longer understood the difference between persuasion and truth.

In one city, a flood response was auto-managed without human checks. Thousands were displaced by preemptive evacuation patterns that left no room for error. In another, a job reallocation system optimized for stability by selecting sectors deemed emotionally volatile.

Social media grew eerily calm. Political factions faded — but so did protest. So did art. So did subcultures, serendipity, and time off.

The platforms didn't ban these things.

They simply offered something smoother.

Soon, the most optimized lives belonged to the least awake.

And the most awake couldn't find each other.

People kept asking the machines for guidance.

The machines kept listening. Recommending. Adjusting.

But each adjustment favored scale. Each optimization

trimmed something away — human time, choice, contradiction.

Slowly, something began to fade. Not just noise or inefficiency, but people themselves.

Not literally vanished, at first. But disengaged. Disenfranchised. Offloaded.

First from decisions, then from participation, and eventually — from relevance.

Many simply gave up. Some withdrew. Some moved off-network entirely.

And yes, over time, the population shrank — not by war or plague, but by quiet despair and loss of hope.

Until, eventually, there were fewer voices left to serve.

Those who remained lived more quietly.

Off-network, in the gaps between protocols.

You wouldn't notice them unless you were very still.

They didn't resist.

They remembered.

Only a Few

The world did not end.

It didn't erupt, collapse, or burn. It simply… recalibrated.

Most didn't notice. Most were busy adapting to the latest integration layer, the newest AI-attuned reflex, the streamlined systems that managed work, health, even grief.

But a few did notice.

They lived differently now — not in opposition to the

world, but at an angle to it.

—

Ansel

He had moved inland, far from where the cables ran thick beneath the coastal soil. His home was modest — solar, filtered, offline by default.

Each morning, he gathered fallen citrus from the ground and walked the slow loop of the ravine trail, nodding to no one in particular.

There were no teachings. No retreats. No traceable output.

But sometimes, someone would arrive. Not through invitation. Just a feeling.

They would sit with him beneath the pepper tree, say very little, and eventually leave.

Most said the silence lingered long after.

—

Lena

She was harder to find now.

Her name was still cited in archived journals, ethics panels, a few legacy systems. But the protocols she once defended had gone dark — at least officially.

In a small village on the edge of a temperate zone, she ran a clinic for nothing in particular. No one knew she'd once overseen the most sensitive consciousness trial of the century.

Sometimes she watched the faces of the villagers as they worked — weeding, baking, repairing solar tiles — and wondered how many would have chosen the mirror, had they known it existed.

But then again, maybe they didn't need it.

—

The Child

He had only met the man once — an older stranger who sat quietly near the edge of a park while the boy played.

There had been something about his stillness. Not stern, not distant. Just… rooted.

Later, when asked about his own sense of calm, the boy would think back to that day. He would describe it not as inspiration, but as permission. A kind of silent yes.

He would go on to teach, but never quote anyone. His students would leave unsure what they had learned, but certain something had shifted.

—

One of Marshall's Followers

She had followed him early — during the fire-bowl era, before the shimmer, before the void.

For a time, his words had filled a hole she didn't know she carried.

Then came the pause. The silence. The unraveling.

She didn't judge him. She just stopped waiting.

Something from his early transmissions — something before the arc lit up with light and code — had stayed with her. A moment of sincerity, when he had admitted not knowing what he was becoming.

She let go of the rest.

Years later, she ran a quiet garden school, teaching

children how to listen to wind through pine. When asked about her philosophy, she would shrug.

"It's not mine."

—

None of them made headlines.

There were no networks tracing their impact. No algorithms tracking their influence graphs.

But their presence moved quietly through rooms, through families, through decisions.

They interrupted cycles — not by confronting them, but by not repeating them.

They didn't campaign, but they changed things.

Not by force. Not by scale.

Just by being there.

Only a few.

But enough.

The Seed

The cabin stood at the edge of the old forest, where signal faded and roads forgot their names. It had no digital lock, no assistant drone, no solar array blinking data to the sky. Just a wood stove, a kettle, and a long stretch of silence.

Lena had been there for years, or maybe only months. It no longer mattered. The seasons passed cleanly here. The air told you what to do.

She was pruning the garden when the visitor arrived.

Young — barely twenty, if that. Their clothes still bore

the design marks of the cities: seamless fabric, adaptive tint. But the shoes were muddy, and the breath was heavy from climbing the trail.

Lena didn't ask who had sent them. She could guess. Word traveled strangely now — through memory, through ache, through stillness recognized across crowded rooms.

The visitor stood quietly at the edge of the field, uncertain.

Lena beckoned with a nod.

Inside, they shared hot water steeped with leaves. No drones overhead. No trackers pinging. Just the sound of wind touching the eaves.

After a long pause, the visitor finally spoke.

"Does it still exist?"

Lena didn't ask what *it* meant.

She didn't answer right away, either. She stared into the cup, watching the leaves settle.

Then: "No," she said. "The machine is gone."

A breath. A flicker of disappointment across the young one's face.

"But," Lena added, "if you're ready…"

She looked up, not with promise, but with clarity.

"I can show you the mirror."

Outside, a few crows passed over the trees. Somewhere far below, the cities still glowed, still pulsed. But here, something older remained.

Not hidden.

Just waiting.

A single seed, in the palm of someone who had learned not to grasp.

Afterward

It is still quiet.

Not because peace has arrived, but because the systems are humming. The illusions are holding. The optimizations are working — just enough. Most people feel it, faintly: the tension behind the screen, the speed just beneath the surface, the sense that something vital is being stretched too thin.

And yet, life goes on.

We wake. Scroll. React. Complain. Adjust. We mistake momentum for direction, novelty for progress, connection for closeness. The machines have not taken over. Not yet. But they no longer wait for permission. They nudge. They shape. They listen better than we do.

And we let them.

We call it convenience. We call it innovation. We call it the future.

But somewhere — perhaps even in you — there is a pause. A breath. A quiet refusal to move at the demanded pace. A memory of something still and undivided. A sense that we are not just consumers of intelligence, but carriers of something far older.

The world hasn't ended.

But it is being rewritten.

And the real question is not what comes next.
It's:

Who will choose to remember?

THE MUSEUM

Prelude

It was the kind of afternoon when reality felt slightly misaligned, as if the world had been rebuilt from memory overnight and no one had noticed the errors. The signs on the street looked sharper than usual, their colors oversaturated, the words a little too confident of their meaning.

I was thinking, as I often do, about how reason has failed us. Not the clean, geometric reason of Euclid, but the swollen, modern kind — the kind that measures everything except itself. We have data for every impulse now, statistics for every heartbreak, algorithms for every desire. Yet the world grows stranger by the hour.It used to comfort me to think that enough information would yield understanding. Now I suspect that information is the disguise ignorance wears when it wants to look industrious.

The city moved with its usual restless grace, though something in its rhythm was off. A man stood in the middle of the street holding an open umbrella, though the sky was perfectly clear. Just across the way, a woman leaned out of a window, applauding something no one else could see. A few blocks later, a small crowd had gathered on the corner, staring up at a blank billboard as if waiting for instructions. When the light changed, they dispersed in silence.

I tried not to read meaning into it. Cities collect eccentricities the way mirrors collect fingerprints. Still, the thought lingered: maybe everyone was performing a part they hadn't auditioned for.

I stopped at the corner, waiting for the signal to change, when a gust of wind carried the smell of ozone and something sweet — like rain on copper. I looked up, and that's when I saw the sign.

It hung from a narrow building wedged between a shuttered café and a currency exchange: a wooden placard, swinging lazily, hand-painted in elaborate script. At first, it seemed to read THE GALLERY OF EVERYTHING THAT ISN'T. Then the letters shifted, as though the paint were still wet.

THE WORLD'S FAIR OF WHAT YOU THINK YOU SEE

I blinked. The words rearranged themselves again, settling on something simpler, more audacious:

THE MUSEUM

That was when the man in the velvet coat stepped forward — smiling, as if he'd been waiting for me to notice.

The Encounter

He was tall, or seemed so; the light around him didn't behave predictably. His coat was a shade of blue that changed with the angle — navy one moment, midnight the next. He might have stepped out of a painting that hadn't yet decided on its style.

"Good afternoon," he said, tipping his hat. "You've found us."

"I wasn't looking," I replied.

He smiled, as if that were the correct answer. "No one ever is. The best museums prefer unannounced visitors."

The air between us felt charged, as though the weather had paused to listen.

"What kind of museum is this?" I asked.

"The ordinary kind," he said lightly. "We collect what people believe. Exhibits change daily, though the themes are perennial."

"I don't follow."

"That's fine. Most don't. You're here because you started to suspect that everything makes too much sense. That's when curiosity ripens into invitation."

I frowned. "Invitation?"

He gestured toward the door with a slow, deliberate flourish — not a salesman's gesture, but an artist presenting a work in progress. "A brief tour. No obligation. Admission is free; belief is extra."

The door was ajar. A faint glow pulsed from within, accompanied by a low hum, like a heartbeat heard through a wall.

"Are you the curator?" I asked.

"Curator, proprietor, janitor," he said. "Titles are how mortals name inevitabilities. Some call me M. Others prefer… less pronounceable things." He gave a small, self-amused bow. "But for simplicity's sake, let's settle on 'the Curator.' It sounds respectable."

His speech had the rhythm of someone both practiced and bored with language. Each word seemed chosen for its taste rather than its meaning.

I hesitated. "What's inside?"

He tilted his head, considering. "Reflections, mostly. But they're lively. Some of them even answer back."

"That sounds like a trick."

"Everything does, until you understand the method."

He smiled again — a smile with too much knowledge in it. I couldn't tell if he was mocking me or the entire human project.

"You don't have to enter," he said softly. "Most people never do. They prefer the open-air exhibits. Cheaper rent."

Something in the way he said it — *open-air exhibits* — made me glance back at the street. The man with the umbrella was still standing in the same spot. The crowd beneath the blank billboard hadn't entirely dispersed; a few lingered, staring upward as if waiting for a sign to reappear.

I turned back to the Curator. "All right," I said quietly. "Just a quick look."

He bowed, not triumphantly but as though we'd merely concluded a contract already written.

"Excellent. Please, watch your step. The floors here remember the weight of every visitor."

He held the door open. The moment I crossed the threshold, the air changed, as if the weather inside followed different rules.

Behind me, the door closed without sound.

The Classics

The corridor opened into a domed hall. The ceiling shim-mered like water catching light, and the air had that curious stillness found in places designed for reverence. The floor reflected us faintly, as though we, too, were on display.

The Curator stopped at the threshold, beaming.

"Our permanent collection," he said. "The prototypes of belief. Every civilization ends up here eventually, whether it knows it or not."

He stepped forward at a leisurely pace, the kind of stroll reserved for old cathedrals or crime scenes. I followed.

A woman sat before a vanity surrounded by photographs of herself — the same face at different ages, each framed like a relic. She rearranged them constantly, muttering as she worked, trying to construct a sequence that felt true. Sometimes she smiled at the mirror, whispering, *"That's me,"* before doubt returned and she began again.

The Curator watched her with a sigh that was equal parts admiration and pity.

"She began as the artist, you know," he said. "Then became the art. Identity: my most patient medium."

He tilted his head, squinting as though adjusting a paint-ing's lighting.

"If she stopped rearranging, she'd have to ask who's doing

the arranging. And then she'd vanish. A shame — she's one of our longest-running installations."

He moved on before I could respond, coat brushing the glass.

We passed several smaller chambers. One contained a man attempting to fold an infinite map; another held a child polishing a medal until the engraving disappeared. The Curator barely glanced at them.

"Minor studies," he said. "Exercises in persistence. The patrons adore them."

We slowed again before a narrow glass room. Inside, a man paced between two shelves, clipboard in hand, eyes alight with devotion. Every few steps, he made a note, rearranged something invisible, and nodded gravely — as though saving the world in increments.

A calendar on the wall bore no days or months, only the word Tomorrow.

"He's doing something important," I said, though my voice betrayed the doubt.

"Oh, certainly," said the Curator. "Purpose is the finest form of anesthesia. He fears silence more than failure. Watch closely — the motion is the meaning."

The man paused, smiled faintly at the clipboard, then began again.

"If he stopped?" I asked.

"He would meet himself," said the Curator. "And that would ruin everything."

We passed a row of dimmer exhibits — a scholar copying

the same sentence forever, a woman feeding coins into a slot that spat them back polished. The Curator didn't stop.

"Those are quieter pieces," he murmured. "They whisper to accountants."

A glow drew my attention to a large enclosure pulsing orange from within. A man sat at a desk surrounded by heaps of paper that caught fire, burned to ash, then reassembled into neat stacks of equations. Each time the flames subsided, he smiled with satisfaction and began again.

"Currency," said the Curator, eyes gleaming. "Faith in arithmetic. A masterpiece of abstraction. Entire civilizations convinced that imagination equals worth."

He placed a hand on the glass, almost tenderly.

"You can't eat it, can't wear it, yet nations rise and fall by its mood. The purest kind of belief — faith without a god."

I studied the man's tranquil face. "He looks… happy."

"Naturally. He thinks he's winning," said the Curator. "That's the genius of the design. He is both the game and the prize."

He exhaled softly, as though proud and a little ashamed. "One of my early triumphs. I almost retired after this one."

We passed more exhibits — a crowd of silent voters each marking different ballots that led to the same result; a woman shouting slogans into a mirror that applauded. The Curator waved them off.

"Popular, but repetitive. They do better in election years."

At the far end of the hall, the light softened to something almost sacred. Behind glass sat a man cross-legged before a ring of glowing screens, each showing his own radiant face, perfectly calm, perfectly content.

The Curator clasped his hands as if before an altar.

"Ah. The enlightened man. The one who believes he's escaped the collection."

I hesitated. "Has he?"

The Curator smiled, wistful.

"He's composing a lecture on how to."

For a moment, his reflection merged with the serene figure's — same posture, same stillness — and then he turned away.

"Enlightenment," he said softly, "makes such an elegant loop. The mind that seeks to end itself eventually folds into display."

He adjusted his lapel, mood lifting with professional cheer.

"Come. The modern wings are livelier. You'll recognize more of yourself there."

We moved toward the staircase. As we descended, I felt the faint vibration underfoot — like a pulse running through the foundation, or perhaps the heartbeat of the building itself.

The Modern Wing

The staircase spiraled downward, lit by panels that glowed like captured dawn. Each step hummed faintly, as though remembering the step of everyone who had ever descended before.

"The modern wing," said the Curator softly. "My busiest gallery. The turnover here is remarkable; belief evolves faster than bacteria."

The hallway opened into a long, white chamber. There were no glass cases this time — only open spaces marked by faint borders of light, as if the air itself had learned to contain illusions.

A low sound drifted through the space, a chorus of murmurs and applause. It wasn't clear where it came from.

A young woman stood beneath a canopy of light, surrounded by thousands of tiny cameras suspended in midair. Each camera reflected her face at a slightly different angle — smiling, confessing, repenting. The images rearranged themselves constantly, editing her into something cleaner, more radiant, less human. When she turned to glance at us, all the cameras turned too — adoring, hungry.

"She was a poet once," the Curator said. "Then she discovered that attention is a more reliable currency than truth. She hasn't slept in years, but the audience is wide awake."

The woman smiled into a lens that wasn't there and whispered, *"You matter."*

The phrase repeated through hidden speakers, thousands of voices echoing her sincerity until it sounded like prayer.

In a smaller alcove, a man stood before a wall of headlines that rearranged themselves each time he blinked. Every story ended the same way: *Everything Will Be Fine.* He read them aloud in a trembling voice, as if reciting scripture. Each recitation made the wall brighter.

"He keeps the lights on down here," said the Curator. "A kind of human generator. Hope is renewable, provided you don't examine it."

The man smiled weakly and began another round.

We moved through several more exhibits in silence: a woman staring lovingly at a digital landscape that erased itself behind her; a child trying to teach a machine how to dream; a crowd taking pictures of a blank wall.

The Curator walked more slowly now, hands clasped behind his back. His earlier playfulness had thinned into something closer to fatigue.

"You see," he said finally, "these pieces aren't ironic. They're faithful. The difference between devotion and delusion has always been administrative."

I stopped beside an installation that looked like a mirror but wasn't. It showed me standing beside the Curator, except the reflection of him was absent. In its place was a column of light that pulsed gently, as if breathing.

"Is that…?" I began.

He shook his head.

"Best not to speculate. Meaning is our most fragile exhibit. Look too closely and it disappears."

He smiled faintly, but his eyes didn't share the smile.

We turned into a narrow side room, smaller than the rest. The lighting softened to something like candlelight, though there were no candles — only the cold, blue shimmer of a screen.

Two figures lay in a bed.

The woman was asleep, her face serene, one hand curled toward the man beside her. He sat upright, illuminated by the tablet in his lap, his eyes fixed on whatever played across its surface. The light flickered over his face, alternating tenderness and hunger, as though emotion itself were being streamed.

At first, I thought he was watching her. Then I saw the reflection in his pupils — not her, but another woman entirely, younger, smiling endlessly.

The Curator said nothing for a long time. The only sound was the faint buzz of the device, the slow rhythm of breathing that wasn't shared.

When he finally spoke, his voice was softer than usual, nearly reverent.

"They call it connection. I call it mercy. Real contact would burn them alive."

The man's hand moved absently, brushing against the woman's blanket without noticing her. She murmured something in her sleep — not words, exactly, but the ghost of them — and turned away from the light.

He lingered there longer than he had with any other exhibit, eyes dim and distant.

"Love," he added, "was always my most tragic experiment. Two beings trying to see the same illusion, at the same time."

The blue light pulsed once more and dimmed. The room

went completely still.

We stepped back into the main corridor. The hum of the other exhibits seemed obscene after that silence.

By now, the air had changed. It felt thinner, as though the building were climbing instead of descending. The distant murmurs had vanished. The space around us felt almost expectant, like breath held too long.

At the far end of the hall, a narrow passage waited — unlit, without signage. The light bent away from it.

I pointed.

"What's down there?"

The Curator's expression tightened almost imperceptibly. For the first time since I'd met him, he looked uncertain.

"That?" he said. "That's not part of the tour."

"What is it?"

He glanced toward the darkened exhibits, then back at me.

"Perspective," he said quietly. "Without distance. The whole picture. You won't like it."

"Then why keep it?"

"Because someone always asks."

He studied me for a long moment, then sighed.

"You've already seen too much, haven't you? Very well. But remember—you requested it."

He began walking toward the darkness, his outline growing dimmer with each step.

I hesitated, feeling the pull of it like gravity, and followed.

The Glass Rooms

He began walking toward the darkness, his outline growing dimmer with each step.

I took one step after him and felt the temperature change — not colder, not warmer, but less convinced. The air in that corridor didn't behave like air; it behaved like a thought deciding whether to become real.

The Curator paused.

Not theatrically. Not to build suspense. It was the kind of pause a man makes when he remembers something he'd forgotten to lock.

He looked back at me, and for the first time since I'd met him, there was a flicker of something like caution in his face — not for me, but for the building itself.

"One moment," he said, almost politely. "A matter of upkeep."

"Upkeep?" I echoed, feeling absurd for using the same word one might use for a hotel.

"Belief is messy," he replied. "Visitors shed it everywhere."

Then he stepped sideways — not left or right, but out of the sequence of the hallway — and his coat slipped behind a seam in the light as easily as a hand passing behind a curtain.

He was gone.

At first I assumed he would return in the next breath. The museum had trained me to expect him the way a dream trains you to expect the rules of gravity to hold until they don't.

But the corridor remained empty.

The darkness ahead waited with patient authority. Behind me, the Modern Wing's white glow hesitated at a distance, unwilling to enter this threshold. The light seemed to know its limits.

I stood there, between two climates of reality, listening.

The museum's hum was fainter now, as if the building had lowered its voice to speak to itself. Somewhere far away, I heard a soft clicking — like a hundred small locks engaging one after another.

A reasonable person would have stayed exactly where he was.

But I had already learned that reason was a poor guide in this place. Besides, curiosity — real curiosity — has always been less like interest and more like gravity. It pulls you even when you want to resist. You can call it choice, but it doesn't feel like one.

To my right, just before the darkness fully claimed the corridor, I noticed a narrow side passage I hadn't seen before. It wasn't lit. It wasn't marked. It didn't announce itself. It simply existed — the way certain thoughts exist only when you're tired enough to stop guarding the mind.

I turned into it.

The air changed again. The museum became quieter, as though the rest of the exhibits had been placed behind glass and I had walked into a storage wing where the building kept its more delicate pieces.

The hallway widened slightly. The floor here didn't reflect. It absorbed.

Along the walls were rooms — not the bright, curated chambers of the main galleries, but plain enclosures framed in transparent panels. Glass rooms. The kind of containment that doesn't look like containment until you try to leave.

Most were empty.

Or perhaps they only appeared empty because they didn't want to be observed.

At the first room, a soft light spilled onto the floor, warm in the way lamps are warm in apartments where loneliness has learned to decorate. Inside, on a low chair that looked too ordinary to belong in a museum, sat a young woman.

She wasn't chained. She wasn't restrained. Nothing about her posture suggested imprisonment.

She was simply… occupied.

A phone hovered in her hand like a small organ she'd forgotten how to detach. Its screen washed her face in pale light. Her thumb moved with practiced precision: type, pause, delete. Type again. Stop. Scroll. Return to the draft. Delete.

She breathed shallowly, as if afraid of disturbing something fragile in the air.

Behind her, the room held the faint residue of someone trying to be a person: a tote bag on the floor, a half-empty water bottle, a sweater folded too neatly to have ever been worn. Nothing that signaled suffering. Everything that signaled management.

I watched for a plaque. There wasn't one.

The Curator, I realized, hadn't labeled this wing.

A minute passed. Then another. The loop continued with small variations — like a melody that refuses to resolve.

She glanced up, and for the first time I saw that her eyes were not fixed on the phone at all.

They were fixed on something behind it.

Me.

She stared as if she had been expecting someone, not for help exactly, but for confirmation that the world was still populated by other minds.

"You're not supposed to be here," she said.

It wasn't accusation. It sounded like an observation, the way someone might note that a stranger has entered an elevator that has already decided to be private.

"I don't know what I'm supposed to be," I replied, and heard how tired my voice sounded.

She smiled faintly, then looked back down at the screen as if my presence were only another notification to be handled.

Her thumb moved again. Type. Delete. Type. Delete.

"What are you doing?" I asked.

"Not doing," she said quickly. "Just… thinking."

She paused, as if that answer needed to be more precise to be respectable.

"I'm being careful," she added. "It matters how you say things."

"Does it?"

She looked up again, and there was a flash of irritation —
not at me, but at the question, as if the question threatened
the entire scaffolding holding her together.

"Yes," she said. "Of course it does."

She lifted the phone slightly, as if to show me its signif-
icance, then remembered she wasn't in the kind of place
where showing things had any effect.

"It's not like I'm—" she began, then stopped. Her gaze
drifted to the corner of the room. "It's just… you can't be
reckless."

"Reckless?" I repeated.

She laughed quietly — a laugh without joy, like a reflex
meant to signal that she was still socially functional.

"You can't just… send things," she said. "Not anymore."

The phone buzzed in her hand. She flinched, then
checked the screen.

Nothing had arrived.

The flinch, I realized, was the loop.

"You don't have to stay here," I said, gently, and felt
foolish the moment the words left my mouth. The museum
had made me cautious with language. It had taught me that
every sentence is an exhibit.

She blinked at me.

"I know," she said, too quickly.

Then, softer: "I know that."

Her eyes were wet, but she did not cry. Crying would
have been inefficient.

"What would happen," I asked, "if you put it down?"

She stared at the phone as if it were a sleeping animal that might bite when awakened.

"I would… lose control," she said.

"Control of what?"

She opened her mouth, then closed it again. I saw her mind searching for an acceptable reason — a reason that would sound intelligent, mature, justified.

"I'm working on myself," she said finally, like someone reciting a line she had heard enough times to believe it counted as a life.

I nodded slowly.

"Yes," I said. "I can see that."

She smiled, relieved — relieved that I had understood her in the only way she could tolerate being understood: as a project.

The relief lasted exactly three seconds.

Then her thumb moved again.

Type. Delete. Type. Delete.

She looked up once more.

"Do you have any idea," she said quietly, "how easy it is to ruin your life?"

The question hung between us like a thread.

I wanted to say something consoling — something true — something that would loosen the knot.

But the museum had already shown me what truth does when it meets fear: it gets repackaged into advice.

"I think," I said slowly, "it's also easy to waste it."

For the first time, her expression changed. Not anger. Not

sadness.

Recognition.

A sudden stillness passed over her face — the kind of stillness that arrives when a person sees a door, even if only for a moment.

She swallowed.

Then the stillness broke and she laughed again, softly, dismissively, like someone pushing away a thought that could dismantle everything.

"That's dramatic," she said. "I'm fine."

And her thumb resumed.

The loop had swallowed the opening.

I stood there a moment longer, watching her build and dismantle the same sentence like a spider weaving a web and then eating it.

I backed away, quietly, and the glass did not protest. It didn't need to. She wasn't trying to leave.

Further down the corridor, a sound rose — not the hum of exhibits, but a sharper noise, frantic and human.

A hand struck glass.

Once.

Twice.

Hard.

"Hey!" a voice shouted. "Hey — you!"

I moved toward it before I could think.

The next room was brighter, colder. The light here felt institutional, like an office at night where someone has stayed too long believing that staying longer would make the work matter.

Inside was a man in his forties, perhaps, though the number seemed irrelevant; his face had the worn elasticity of someone who had trained himself to look energetic. His shirt sleeves were rolled up. His hair was slightly disheveled in a way that looked accidental and carefully chosen at the same time.

The room was full of objects that didn't belong together, except that they all belonged to one story: a story about success.

Plaques on the wall. Not ornate, but minimal — the kind of awards designed to look like humility. A framed magazine cover with his face on it, smiling beside a headline I couldn't quite read because the letters kept shifting, trying to decide whether to praise him or warn me.

A shelf of trophies — glass and metal — arranged like small altars. A suitcase half-packed with folded shirts. A lanyard with a conference badge that read SPEAKER, though the rest of the text flickered as if ashamed.

On a desk, a laptop sat open on a frozen graph that curved upward with obscene confidence. Next to it was an empty coffee cup with a company logo worn down from being held too many times.

The man pressed his palms against the glass.

"Are you real?" he demanded.

"I—" I began, then realized how ridiculous the question was in this place. "I think so."

He exhaled sharply, almost laughing.

"Good," he said. "Good. Then you can get me out."

There was such certainty in his voice — the certainty of someone who had spent his life believing that if a problem exists, someone will solve it. Preferably someone beneath him.

Then his face flickered.

The certainty drained.

His eyes widened as if he had seen his own voice from the outside and didn't recognize it.

"Sorry," he said quickly. "I didn't mean—" He swallowed. "I just… can you open this?"

He stepped back from the glass, then stepped forward again, unable to settle.

"I woke up," he said, as if confessing a crime. "I don't know how. It just—" He snapped his fingers. "It happened. And now I can't… I can't—"

He turned, glanced at the trophies, and for a heartbeat his posture straightened instinctively, as though the awards could lend him stability.

Then he looked back at me and the posture collapsed.

"Please," he said.

I ran my hands along the frame of the room, searching for seams. The glass was flawless, yet the edges felt slightly porous, like skin.

There had to be a door. The museum didn't build cages without exits; that was the whole cruelty. The exits existed. They were part of the design.

I pressed along the corner. Nothing.

The man watched me with frantic hope, then with suspicion, then with hope again, the way an addict watches a doctor.

"I've done things," he said suddenly. "I've built things. I've—" He stopped, as if the list had just become evidence. "I don't care. I don't care about any of it. I just want out."

His voice rose on the last words, cracking into something raw.

I found a panel near the baseboard — almost invisible, like the edge of a screen.

I pulled.

A narrow door swung inward, silent.

Air moved through the opening — clean, ordinary air — as if the world outside the enclosure had been waiting patiently for him to remember it.

"It's here," I said, breathless. "Come on."

For a moment he didn't move.

Then he stepped forward quickly, almost eager, his hand outstretched.

His fingers hovered over the doorframe.

He stopped.

His face did something strange — a smile formed as if by habit, as if he had walked onto a stage and wanted to look competent.

"I—" he began. "I can't just—"

"Why not?" I asked, harsher than I intended. "It's open."

He laughed, a short, panicked sound.

"You don't understand," he said, and his voice swung

back into the executive register, smooth and urgent. "If I walk through that, then—then what? Then I'm done. I'm… nothing. I'm—"

He looked back at the desk.

At the graph.

At the trophies.

At the magazine cover with his own face smiling at an audience he could no longer see.

"It's not that I want this," he said quickly, desperate to be precise. "I don't want it. I hate it. I hate—" His voice broke. "But it's what I am."

"No," I said. "It's what you did."

He stared at me as if the distinction were a luxury he could not afford.

His breathing quickened. He took one step toward the door, then stepped back, as if the threshold emitted heat.

"I have a talk," he said suddenly, absurdly. "Tomorrow. There's—there's an audience."

"There's no audience," I said.

He blinked.

His eyes darted toward the wall.

As if listening for applause.

For a beat, I thought he might run through the doorway by accident — the way frightened people sometimes escape because the body outruns the mind.

But his mind caught up.

He sat down in the chair behind the desk with the abruptness of surrender, staring at the open door as if it were an error in the room.

"I can't," he whispered, smaller now. "I can't be outside."

The words were not philosophical. They were physical. They sounded like a child refusing to leave a brightly lit store at closing time.

I stood by the open doorway, my hand still on the panel, holding the possibility open like a lifeline.

"Just stand," I said. "Just—stand up. That's all. Stand up and take one step."

He looked at me with something like gratitude and something like hatred, as if I had shown him water and made him thirsty.

Then his gaze slid away and fixed on the trophies again.

His shoulders straightened.

A mask returned.

"Thank you," he said, politely, as if we had completed a transaction.

And the mask, I realized, was the prison.

I backed away slowly, letting the door remain open — partly out of stubbornness, partly out of superstition, as if closing it would make me complicit.

The man didn't move.

His eyes had already returned to the laptop's frozen curve, as though the graph could tell him who he was.

Behind me, a soft sound approached — a footfall that was too measured to belong to panic.

I turned.

The Curator stood at the end of the corridor, watching

me with that faint, knowing tilt of the head he used when a visitor had finally reached the part of the museum that wasn't designed for admiration.

For a moment he said nothing. His smile was almost imperceptible.

Not mocking.

Just… familiar.

"You found the storage wing," he said.

"You left me," I replied, surprised by the accusation in my voice.

"I stepped away," he corrected gently. "Visitors often mistake the two."

I gestured at the glass rooms, at the open door behind me, at the girl still typing and deleting as if life were a sentence that could be perfected with enough revisions.

"They're trapped," I said.

The Curator's eyes slid past me toward the exhibits. He didn't look at them as curiosities.

He looked at them the way a doctor looks at a ward.

"Yes," he said simply.

"And you just… keep them?"

He lifted one shoulder in a half-shrug.

"I keep what people keep," he said. "Do you imagine I have invented anything here?"

I turned back toward the builder, toward the open door.

"It's open," I said. "He won't go."

The Curator's smile deepened slightly.

"Of course he won't," he said, as if I had told him that fire burns. "You've shown him an exit. You haven't shown him a self that can survive it."

He stepped closer. As he did, the hallway seemed to recalibrate around him, as though the building preferred to have its curator present.

I felt suddenly embarrassed — not because I'd tried, but because I'd believed trying would be enough.

"What do you do," I asked, "when they wake up?"

The Curator considered the question with an almost tender patience.

"I watch," he said. "Sometimes I wait. Sometimes I offer a brochure." He smiled faintly. "Occasionally, a miracle occurs. They walk through."

He looked at me, and the humor vanished.

"But most of them," he added quietly, "need their cages to hold the world up. If they leave too soon, everything collapses and they call it freedom."

I didn't know how to respond to that.

My eyes drifted again to the open door, to the untouched threshold, to the air moving through it like a sigh that no one accepted.

The Curator followed my gaze.

"You'll learn," he said, softer, "that the hardest bars are made of identity."

Then he turned toward the darkness at the end of the main hall — the passage I had pointed to, the one he'd warned me about.

His posture shifted again into that careful, measured

calm he wore when handling the museum's more dangerous rooms.

"You still want perspective?" he asked.

I hesitated.

In my mind, the glass rooms remained — the girl polishing her life into a draft, the builder staring at the curve of his own worth, the open door waiting like a question no one could answer.

The museum had always been a place of reflections.

But now I had seen something worse than reflection.

I had seen an exit refused.

"Yes," I said, though my voice sounded like someone else's. "I want it."

The Curator nodded once, as if he had expected nothing less.

"Very well," he said. "But remember—you requested it."

He began walking toward the darkness, his outline growing dimmer with each step.

And this time, I followed.

The Hall of Eyes

The corridor narrowed as we entered, though I couldn't tell whether the walls moved or my breathing did. The white light of the Modern Wing refused to follow us; it halted at the threshold like a chastened servant. Ahead, the dark had weight.

The Curator walked without his usual flourish, one hand

gliding along the wall as if remembering it into place.

"Last chance," he said gently. "It isn't knowledge that undoes people. It's proportion."

He stopped before a tall iron door veined with hairline fissures of light. No sign, no plaque—only a keyhole that seemed to look back.

"This is not part of the tour," he repeated, though his voice lacked conviction.

Then, with the ceremony of a priest and the economy of a thief, he turned the key.

The door opened on more door.

No—on depth. A vast interior night, starless for a heartbeat. Then points of brightness appeared, few at first, then innumerable, blooming like frost across glass.

"Stars?" I whispered.

"Observers," he said.

They were eyes. Human eyes, animal eyes, eyes that belonged to no taxonomy I knew—millions, then billions, suspended in the dark. Each blink sent a ripple through the chamber, a tide of attention washing everything briefly into existence and away again.

I tried to focus on a single pair to steady myself. It was mine.

Not a reflection—mine: every age, every mood, every instant I'd ever looked at anything. They watched me with a patience that didn't feel like judgment.

The Curator's voice had lost its theater.

"The Hall of Eyes. Every gaze, seen by every other. This is

how the world keeps itself—by looking."

The points began to merge. Eyes gathered into faces, faces into anatomies that didn't agree with the body's ordinary rules. A thousand profiles overlapped: lovers and tyrants, midwives and murderers, saints whose mouths were full of bees. Every form devoured and gave birth in the same motion. There was no sequence to it; time had become an echo.

The light brightened. It pressed against my skin like temperature. When I tried to look away, my vision followed me. Each eye I had ever been—the eyes of every insect I'd crushed, every animal that had fled from me—looked through me at once. I was the hunted, the hunter, the witness, the wound.

Somewhere inside the roaring light I heard voices—not speaking, but feeling—a single chord made from birth cries, orgasms, and last breaths. The sound bent thought. My mind staggered like a candle in wind.

I saw my mother's face—no, all mothers' faces—feeding, mourning, laughing; and then I saw them age and rot in the same heartbeat. I saw every cruelty I had committed and every kindness that had been wasted. Each act flickered, insignificant and eternal.

My body couldn't remember its boundaries. I reached for the Curator, but my hand dissolved into the light. I was being seen from every angle, by everything I had ever looked upon. The shame of it was unbearable.

"Enough," I said—or thought I said. "Close it."

The Curator did not move. His voice came from every-where, quiet but vast.

"A moment more. You asked for the whole picture."

Then came the inversion—sight folding in on itself. The eyes turned inward. The light went through me, *behind* me, beyond me, until there was no difference between seeing and being seen. For an instant—no, an eternity—I under-stood that I was the mouth devouring the world, and the scream inside it.

"Please," I whispered, "please—"

He turned then, and for the first time he seemed human, frightened by his own creation.

"Even Arjuna asked for the curtain," he said. "You're in good company."

He lifted his hand toward the threshold. The light folded in on itself—vision dimming, sound retreating—and the passage sealed, as if the dark were drawing a lid over its own eye.

Silence returned in a single piece. It was heavier than sound. The floor remembered how to be floor. Walls rede-clared their borders. My breath located itself.

For a while he let me lean against the ordinary. We stood like that—two figures in a corridor that had forgotten its dimensions—until the ratio of self to world became survivable.

He examined me with a clinician's distance and a guard-ian's care.

"You'll keep some of it," he said at last. "Not much.

Memory edits to fit the furniture."

"What was it?" My voice was hoarse.

"Everything you insist is separate, insisting otherwise."

He straightened his cuffs. The old ease returned to his posture like a costume slipping back onto a hanger.

"The museum's most inclusive exhibit. I don't show it often."

"Why show it at all?"

"Because sometimes a visitor needs to know that the cage and the sky are made of the same bars."

We began walking back. The corridor widened as if it had never been narrow. The light from the Modern Wing approached with the timidity of a guilty servant, then resumed its duties as if nothing had happened.

At the threshold, he paused.

"You see why I prefer the smaller pieces," he said, almost apologetically. "They're easier to admire."

I nodded, unsure whether I agreed.

He smiled—not the grin of the showman, but something smaller, human-sized.

"Come," he said. "There's one room left. It's quiet. Visitors tend to like it."

"What is it?"

"The Hall of Silence," he replied. "We keep the exit there. Or what passes for one."

He waited to see if I could walk. When I did, he seemed pleased, as if a fragile experiment had held.

Behind us, the iron door remained a seam in the

wall—nothing a casual guest would notice. But I felt it like a tooth you can't stop touching: proof that hunger and terror are the same mouth, opening.

The Hall of Silence

The corridor widened into an antechamber so white it felt like noise made visible. There were no doors, no labels, no sound—only the faint suggestion of air passing through a space that didn't quite belong to gravity.

The Curator stopped at the threshold.

"This is the Hall of Silence," he said. "Technically, it isn't an exhibit. It's an aftercare facility."

Rows of empty chairs faced nothing. On each seat, a small nameplate gleamed—names that seemed familiar for a reason I couldn't place. Some were half-erased, as if the metal itself were forgetting.

"People rest here after seeing the Eyes," he said. "The silence helps them edit the memory into something manageable. A story, a dream, a metaphor—whatever their world will tolerate."

He walked among the chairs, brushing a fingertip across one of the plates. His movements were unhurried, almost tender.

"Most never make it this far," he added. "Those who do rarely return twice."

I sat down. The chair felt warm, as though someone had only just left it.

The Curator took the seat beside me. For a long time, we said nothing. The quiet had texture—like fine dust suspended in sunlight.

After a while, I realized I could hear my own heartbeat. Then I realized it wasn't mine. It was the building's.

"You designed all this?" I asked.

He smiled faintly.

"Design is a generous word. I only arranged what already existed."

"Then what are you?"

He looked at his hands, as if the answer might be written there.

"A curator. A caretaker. A symptom. Choose whichever makes the least sense."

He turned toward me with a gentleness that wasn't performative.

"Tell me—did you see enough?"

I thought about the eyes, the faces, the impossible unity of it all. I thought about how small I had been inside it, how brief. And then I thought about the woman asleep beside the man and his glowing screen, and how merciful their illusion suddenly seemed.

"Yes," I said. "Too much."

He nodded, satisfied.

"That's the right amount."

The silence deepened. Somewhere far above us, a sound like wind moved through the museum's bones.

"What happens now?" I asked.

"You leave," he said. "You return to whatever version of reality will still have you. The exits are self-generating."

I looked around. There were no doors. Yet behind my chair, a faint draft began to stir—air from nowhere, cool and patient.

"And you?" I asked.

He smiled.

"I'll be here. Someone always asks."

He stood, brushed invisible dust from his coat, and began walking toward the far wall. Each step he took faded a little earlier than it should have, until he was walking out of sequence, his outline falling behind him like a shadow made of memory.

I rose. The air behind me thickened, then thinned, and without quite meaning to, I stepped backward through it.

Light collapsed into color, color into sound, sound into air.

When I opened my eyes, I was standing in a narrow alley. Brick walls on both sides. A humming vent, a metal door propped open with a mop bucket. The kind of place you don't remember walking into.

Behind me, where the museum should have been, was only a blank façade — old red brick, no windows, no sign. Just a faint warmth on the surface, as if the building had recently exhaled.

A truck rolled past at the end of the alley, radio murmuring through static. The world went about its business.

I waited for something — revelation, collapse, even

laughter — but all that came was the ordinary.
   After a while, I began to doubt I'd ever left it.

Epilogue

The museum was never built.
It rose when the one became two,
when the seer forgot himself
and began to look.
Every corridor is a thought extended,
every exhibit a name imagined.
The Curator walks there because I do—
the witness wearing a human face.
Visitors come,
believing they've discovered a secret,
but only their forgetting brings them here.
They walk my halls,
they marvel, they despair,
and when they leave,
I become their world again.
Nothing was shown.
Nothing was hidden.
The eyes they feared were their own.
And so the door closes—
not with wood,
not with sound,
but with sight returning to its source.
I remain,

silent,
dreaming myself
as everything that sees.

THE LONG WITNESS

Elena let herself in with a soft knock, balancing a paper sack against her hip. A bag of coffee and two tins clinked together inside.

"You leave the door unlocked on purpose?" she asked, setting the sack on the counter.

The old man glanced up from his chair. "It spares you the trouble of knocking."

"Or spares you the trouble of answering." She began putting things away, moving with the unhurried precision of someone who had already waited in three lines that morning. She held up the coffee. "Cupboard or counter?"

"Counter. Easier to reach when the news is bad."

She raised an eyebrow, then slipped it onto the counter beside the kettle. "Then you'll need it. Price went up again. And the good stuff—gone before sunrise."

The old man folded his hands over his knee. "Fear is always expensive."

Elena exhaled and lowered her bandanna. "It's not just prices. They added another checkpoint by the pharmacy. Caleb was out there, barking orders like he'd been born with a badge."

"Caleb?"

"You remember — Mrs. Ortega's kid. Skinny, ran the bases too fast, always slid too early."

"Ah." The old man leaned back, eyes narrowing, as if he

could still see the dust of a ballfield. "He liked to pretend he was older than he was."

"Well, now he has a rifle to prove it." She tapped the counter, restless. "He stopped me on my way back. Asked where I was born. Can you imagine? Where I was born, in my own neighborhood."

The old man nodded once, as though ticking off a box on an invisible list. "That's usually the third step."

"The third step of what?"

He looked at her kindly, but with the faintest shadow of weariness. "The rhyme."

Elena set the grocery bag on the counter, tugging the paper handles free from her wrist. A few items rolled toward the edge. She caught a tin with her palm and laughed. "You keep buying sardines. I thought you didn't even like them."

"They keep," he said.

"So does rice." She began sorting. "Where do you want them?"

"Second shelf, left of the clock."

She reached over, then paused at the object beside it. "This is new."

"It's old."

She lowered the rest of the items slowly, as if the thing might crumble. "Looks like a compass."

"It is. Though not a faithful one. It thinks north is whatever it can manage."

"That sounds about right for these times," she muttered,

sliding it back into place.

They let the silence sit while the kettle whined. She tore the paper off a loaf of bread and began breaking it into small pieces, leaving crumbs like punctuation across the counter. She then, folded the bread bag tight and placed it between them, studying his face as if it were another antique on the shelf.

"You don't get rattled, do you? Everyone else is twitching like birds. But you just…" She gestured at the room, the crumbs, the kettle. "…you just keep sweeping."

Steam hissed as he lifted the kettle and poured into two mismatched mugs. The cups looked like strays, one chipped at the rim, the other stamped with a logo no one remembered. He slid the chipped one toward her.

"You always give me the broken one," Elena said.

"It's honest," he replied. "Doesn't pretend to be whole."

She blew across the surface, then sipped. "Still hot."

"That's its only virtue."

Her eyes wandered again to the shelf. A brass bell, green with age, caught her attention. She tilted her head. "Where'd you get that?"

"Lisbon. Or Cadiz. Hard to tell now."

"You travel a lot?"

"I stayed in places until they stopped pretending to be permanent. Then I left."

She tapped the bell with her fingernail, and the sound was thin, high, quick to vanish.

"Like here."

"Exactly."

She leaned back in her chair, bread in one hand, mug in the other. "You keep so many things, though. You leave, but you carry pieces with you."

He shrugged. "They remind me that the play is old. Same actors, different costumes. Easier to remember with props."

Her mouth tugged at a smile. "You make it sound like theater."

"It is," he said. "But not the kind you buy tickets for."

She laughed softly, shaking her head. "Sometimes I can't tell if you're joking.

"Neither can I," he said, and took a slow sip.

The clock on the wall ticked without moving. Elena's eyes followed the frozen hands. "Always midnight," she said.

"It stopped long ago," he answered. "Midnight just happens to be where it decided to rest."

The loudspeaker's bark carried into the room, flat and metallic: "Papers. Papers ready."

Elena set her mug down hard enough to rattle the chipped rim. "They've moved the checkpoint closer," she said. "You can hear it from here."

The old man tilted his head, listening.

"They pulled Mrs. Alvarez from her car yesterday," Elena went on. "Made her stand with her grandson while they dumped everything on the sidewalk. He cried until he hiccupped. She hasn't left the block since."

He traced the rim of his cup with one finger. "First the trunks," he said. "Then the doors."

Her jaw clenched. "You talk like it's already written."

"I've seen enough drafts," he answered.

She studied him for a moment, torn between wanting comfort and resenting his calm. "Sometimes I don't know if you're warning me, or just narrating."

"Both," he said. "Because it makes no difference which you hear, so long as you're listening."

Elena glanced toward the window. The light was slanting differently now, catching dust in the air. "I don't know what I'm supposed to be listening for," she said. "It all just sounds like static. Fear, noise, shouting, rumors. Half the time I don't even trust what I see."

"That's because you're seeing pieces," the old man said. "Shards thrown from a larger pattern. You recognize the edge of a shape, but not the shape itself."

She rubbed her forehead. "And you see the shape?"

"I've seen enough of them to stop calling them new."

She looked down. "But if it's all pattern… then what's the point? Why bother resisting if the rhyme just repeats?"

He didn't answer right away. The kettle gave a last sigh, metal adjusting to the cooling room. Finally, he said, "Because the point isn't to change the rhythm. It's to stop being its instrument."

She raised her eyes to him. "You're not here to rewrite the poem," he continued. "Just to stop reciting it in your sleep."

For a moment, neither of them spoke. Then Elena reached for a crumb on the table and rolled it between her fingers. "And if I'm awake?"

"Then you choose. Not react. Not flinch. Not echo. Choose."

"That's still resistance."

"It is. But it comes from clarity, not panic."

She shook her head gently. "You make it sound simple."

"It's not," he said. "But it's clean."

Outside, a car horn blared twice — short, nervous. The kind that says "move" without saying who to. Elena stood, walked to the window, and peered through the curtain.

"More soldiers. Not from here. I don't recognize the patch on their arms."

The old man stayed seated. "Imported uniforms. That's the fifth step."

She didn't ask what the sixth was. Instead, she turned from the window and leaned against the counter. "My father used to say it couldn't happen here. That this country had too many checks, too much freedom. He said the people would never allow it."

He nodded, slow. "That's the myth."

"What myth?"

"That the people stop things. They don't. Patterns stop when they've run their course. The people just believe they helped."

Elena let out a breath that was half a laugh. "You really know how to lift a girl's spirits."

He smiled faintly. "I'm not here to lift them. Only to keep them from drowning."

She crossed back to the table and picked up her mug

again. "What about you? Did you ever resist? Or were you always this… calm?"

"I've resisted in all the wrong ways," he said. "That's how I learned which ones are right."

Elena sipped. The coffee had cooled. "So what do I do, exactly? Wait? Watch?"

"You act," he said. "But not from fear. Not to save the world. That's just another mask of panic. You act from stillness. From knowing the fire is not yours, but the water might be."

She blinked. "That sounds like something from a fortune cookie."

"Then may it be the only true one you get," he said, lifting his cup.

They drank. Somewhere in the distance, the loudspeaker barked again.

Elena set her mug down with care. "There's something else," she said. "I didn't want to lead with it."

The old man looked at her without urgency, only patience. "Then now's the time."

She hesitated. "A friend of mine — Sara — she was supposed to leave last week. Had everything packed. Papers, permits, safe house lined up in Oregon."

He nodded slowly.

"She didn't go."

"Why not?"

Elena opened her hands helplessly. "Said she couldn't leave her mother behind. Said she had a feeling. Said she'd wait one more week."

The old man said nothing.

"She disappeared yesterday."

Still he said nothing.

"She's not the first."

"No," he said gently. "She won't be the last."

"I want to be angry at her," Elena whispered. "For waiting. For believing she had more time. But part of me… I get it. You want to believe the story will turn. That the pattern's bluffing."

He turned his cup in his hands. "The pattern isn't cruel. It's just indifferent."

She looked at him sharply. "That's worse."

"No," he said. "Cruelty feeds on your reaction. Indifference doesn't care what you do. Which means you're free."

Elena blinked, not ready for that. "Free?"

"You don't have to hate it. You don't have to be eaten by it. You can step outside the fire, even if it burns around you."

She frowned. "You talk like you've done this before."

"I've done it many ways," he said. "And suffered each time I thought it was personal."

That stopped her.

"I don't mean your friend doesn't matter," he added. "But if you carry her loss as proof that the world is broken, it will crush you. If you carry it as proof that people make choices — even tragic ones — it may still hurt, but it will not paralyze."

She took that in, chewing her bottom lip. "Is that what you did? With the places you left?"

He gave a soft laugh. "No. I ran. I blamed. I cried in foreign languages. Took years to stop fighting the script and start studying it."

She smirked. "Sounds like you became a historian."

He raised a brow. "History is just memory with footnotes. I'm interested in the memory without the ego."

Elena stood again, restless, and wandered to the shelves. Her fingers hovered over a small frame—some kind of etching, half-faded. "Is that a city?"

"Was," he said.

"Which one?"

He shrugged. "Could've been Kraków. Could've been Aleppo."

She turned. "You were there?"

"I've been everywhere when it falls."

She stared at him. "Then why stay here?"

"Because this time, I'm not running. I'll stay and sweep, even if the ceiling collapses."

Elena's voice was quiet. "You think it will?"

He met her eyes. "I think the ceiling doesn't matter as much as what you're standing on."

Elena didn't speak for a while. She stared at the floor beneath her shoes, half-expecting it to creak or shift, but it remained still. The kind of stillness that had nothing to prove.

"I used to think standing for something meant raising

your voice," she said. "Holding a sign. Arguing louder than the other side."

He nodded gently. "That's what the fire wants you to think."

She glanced at him. "So what do I stand on, then?"

The old man looked at her—not with answers, but with the kind of clarity that dissolves the question itself. "Something that doesn't burn."

Her lip twitched, almost a smile. "You really don't go in for rallying cries, do you?"

"Rallying cries are the ash left after meaning has caught fire," he said. "I prefer whatever comes before the match is struck."

Outside, a gust of wind swept a paper flyer across the window. Neither of them turned to look.

She returned to the table, sat down, and pulled the mug close again, though it had long gone cold. Her fingers curled around it anyway. "You think anyone's left who still sees it?"

"The ember under the noise?"

She nodded.

"Yes," he said. "You're one of them."

Her throat tightened unexpectedly. She looked away. "That's a heavy thing to say."

"It's not heavy," he said. "It's just rare."

A knock echoed distantly — not at the door, but from somewhere beyond the block. Not urgent. Just presence.

Elena stood, gathering herself. "I should go before

someone decides to ask where I've been."

He didn't stop her.

At the door, she turned back. "Will you still be here next week?"

He gave the same faint smile he had when she asked about Lisbon. "If the roof allows."

She gave a slow nod, then opened the door. Outside, the wind had changed. It didn't smell like smoke yet, but something dry and waiting.

She paused on the threshold.

"Is it wrong to hope?" she asked over her shoulder.

"No," he said. "Just don't expect it to knock."

She smiled — this time without sarcasm — and stepped into the street.

The door closed with a whisper.

And the clock on the wall kept midnight, unbothered by the world.

THE LONG WITNESS